Bridges of Three Rivers

I0525753

Bridges of Three Rivers

Kelly Fields
kelthscreations.blog

Diana Cojocaru – Cover art

Other books by Kelly Fields
Avant-garde
Millennium Earth
Guiding the Stars
Margo's Poems and Songs
Crossing Rivers

ISBN: 978-0-9998820-5-4

Bridges of Three Rivers

Preface

Although growing up in two entirely different environments, they were meant for each other. Life would pose many struggles for both of them. Although she was from an aristocratic lineage, she seemed to reject the wealth of it all. He grew up in hardships, at least financially, and his parents were both immigrants from south of the border. These two were missing many things in this life and finding each other would be the answer to their life struggles. Only life is never easy; they learned this the hard way. Somehow they survived it all after they came in contact with the Masters of their existences. They both had much to learn and lots of burdens to remove from their Spirits. Once they find mindfulness in their inner being, many miracles will start to happen for them.

Her first love betrayed her and she learned he didn't seem to have the right stuff anyway. This was after many years of trying to keep their marriage together. And after all, there were children involved, but what he had done was just something she couldn't tolerate. She would be alone until her mom moved in, but that came with its challenges. New things to try in life would be her goal along with raising the kids, but she grows tired of life's constant circle of one boring thing after another which has to end. Never did she think of suicide because her strong Catholic roots wouldn't allow that.

Bridges of Three Rivers

Growing up without a father wasn't his mother's plan. However, he turned into a fine young man that was a blessing to his mom, and helped guide his younger brother. Working on his grandparent's farm was a teaching example that couldn't be measured in academic terms. With the body completely satisfied with good hard work only left his brain very active. Full of good clean oxygen on the farm, he gravitated to whatever he desired, and he desired to be a doctor.

Was it fate that they met or was it just by chance? She returned to the area where she attended college, and he never really left, at least not for any permanent job. They were both coming to their end of any chances of meeting someone. That is the only love in their lives that had eluded them for all these years. Could they finally find that one love; that one hope or were they going to end their days wondering what if?

Find out what will happen, learn if they find each other, and if they were meant for each other. See what might happen if two people that have given so much for so long meet and share their energies to continue being a blessing on this planet. Could they go further together than they could ever have alone or do they take a well-deserved break from the problems of life? These possibilities are endless and should be explored; they really should be.

In this story, you will discover the many aspects of how society is broken down into different segments. Here, you will also see that many people don't follow *the stereotypes of their status in the economies of life. Instead, many people are very kind and just looking for a way to be helpful. Sometimes it only takes the courage of a person in need to ask them for help. Helping others is the greatest way to find true happiness in this life.*

CHAPTER 1

"Whoa, whoa," she said as the truck was barely staying on the ground for more than two seconds! Bullets were flying all around, some hitting the back, and shattering the window! "Are we going to make it out alive!" she cried as their assailants closed the gap on them. He didn't answer her, he was too busy trying to bandage his friend Shamir's arm that was hit by a stray bullet that whizzed by, and pierced through his shoulder.

He turned to her after performing combat first aide on his friend, and then said "yes we are! I know we are going to make it out of here alive!" Looking around, he suddenly noticed that their assailants were closing the gap! Now after helping to stop the bleeding on his friend's arm, he was ready to stop their advance. Grabbing an AK-47, he quickly put his prior military training to good use, loaded the chamber, and aimed for the advancing truck's radiator.

Ping, ping, tat, tat, tat and then swoosh! The steam was then set free from the radiator, and one of the assailant's three trucks was now out of service, but a second one was approaching the side of their truck. This scene was similar to an old pirate ship trying to board a shipping vessel only to kill and plunder. He would never be ready to surrender, for he knew that they would take no prisoners, or be gentle with his wife. This only meant a fight until they were killed or able to escape!

Quickly he swung around to his left flank and shot out the rear tire of the enemy truck, but two men were able to board the truck anyway as theirs went hobbled, and then flipped over. One of the men swung a machete over, and a glancing blow struck his arm. This blow wasn't fatal because it also hit the butt of his rifle and this caused his reflexes to go into action. Then he lifted his right leg and kicked this thug overboard!

All the while his wife had managed to take over the driving to therefore allow one of the men to join George in defending their group from the marauders. With one of the men struggling with the remaining thug, George was enthralled with laying down a barrage of weapon fire to keep the last enemy truck at bay.

Hurry, hurry! The men yelled at her from the back. They could see that the final truck was well armored and wouldn't be easily stopped. The only saving grace was that because of the heavy armor it was a little slower than the first two that were now out of commission. Knowing this, they were still very hopeful because the gate to their compound was less than 2 kilometers away.

She was doing her best to keep the pedal floored while still trying not to allow the massive ditches in the desert to impede them from reaching the gate. On seeing two clouds of dust leave out of the gate, they knew that help was on the way. Before they could shout out to them these two armored vehicles flew by on each side. Guns blazing at the enemy truck caused the marauders to stop and turn around. Then in their truck they raised their rifles in the air and yelled as their truck dashed past the gate and into the compound!

Once inside the compound, the wounded were taken to the infirmary and given care from their doctor friends. She noticed that her husband's wounded leg was taken care of by one of their colleagues. Then as he turned his cut arm was visible to her! Running to him she quickly helped to finish treating the wounded leg and gently lifted his arm to clean, and bandage it.

Too tired to ask him how it happened, she said to herself *what does it matter anyway? We were in a fight for our lives so to have escaped the torture they had planned for us is sufficient enough to be grateful.* Later that evening they hugged each other, counted their blessings, then crashed for the night, and slept halfway into the next day. It had been a very tiring, trying, and joyful eight months in the middle of nowhere.

Bridges of Three Rivers

Review

Our time here can be divided into three parts, they are all essential in growing our hearts.

Part one is, of course, our beginning at birth, do not push aside this one's worth.

This is where we lose knowledge of who we are and we can't communicate except with our star.

To learn a language from our guardians here, these former travelers, and their love is so dear.

School is their essential indoctrination plan and some things that are taught aren't very grand.

When part one is complete, you will be ready to begin your memorable years, so rock steady.

Part two now starts and your loyalty will form, this is one thing the world calls the norm.

Maybe finding love is what you desire, this is a beautiful thing to aspire.

You both work full time to achieve your dream and this will be the start of walking the beam.

Home is on the checklist as something to buy and you feel this is needed, but don't know why.

Time to paint the third room pink or blue, there is only one reason, and your baby is due.

Bridges of Three Rivers

Your child is ready for school to start, mom will go back to work for her part.

Busy with this life you won't understand that now you are a guardian of the world's plan.

Sports, politics, and religion are now here to teach you to compete, divide, and to fear.

Children are now ready to go to college and learn all that the world will teach them to discern.

Seeing them start to live in part two, your Spirit wonders, what's next to do?

Part three is where a decision is made, to ascend or continue in this world's charade.

Hopefully, you want to ascend to the next level, not doing this could be like following the devil.

That's a tough thing to say I do feel, but to not think this body will die is so unreal.

With only one of two ways to forsake, one is love, and the other is hate.

There aren't a lot of things you need to do, only change your way, and let love shine through.

The heart will open and take in all that's good, then enable you to love because you should.

The day will come when our time is done, then we will ascend back to the Source, and be one.

Before her paradigm shift in life would happen many years later. Somewhere in the metropolis of the world, she would be groomed to take over her daddy's business. Since her mom didn't bear any sons, her daddy accepted that she was the only heir to assume the role as the CEO. This brought a lot of contention for her, since she wasn't too keen on business, especially because it had nothing to do with her passions in life.

So far out in the country, in a tiny little town in Southern Michigan, he would grow up watching a lot of television shows, but never really comprehended what the real world was like. Waking up early to feed the few animals that they had would one day seem like the most beautiful thing in the world, but he didn't understand why they were so poor. He was cooking, cleaning, and watching his little brother; he was undoubtedly a special child. In all things, he would be conscious to help his mom in any way he could.

Being the only child wasn't something that she had thought much about; although having a baby sister was her wish since her youth. Her mom and dad tried to have another child, but it just wasn't in the cards. Many times, her mom would ask her dad about adoption, but every time he had an answer for why not to adopt, and so she decided that he wasn't going to give in. Although he would go away for business deals most of the time, he still seemed to run the household, even from many miles away.

Friends were always plenty, but boyfriends were not on her radar while in grade school. Watching medical shows and volunteering at the hospital became an obsession when she was a teen. Looking back, she wonders if it wasn't an escape from her dad, who was trying to micromanage her life. He would keep on trying to push her into business classes whenever possible, but being away most of the time, he couldn't force her to go for business classes.

Life in this wealthy family wasn't all we would think it was. She felt guilty for the money that her daddy made from his business deals. As she studied them more and more they were not equitable for both sides. Her daddy repeatedly tried to teach her how to take advantage of the consumers by cheating them. Sometimes she wasn't sure if he even realized that they were also human beings.

That's a little background on Shelia Ursula McCormick, though there is no relation to the spice company. His name is George Fernando Esperanza and though they met many years ago, today wasn't the first that time they almost lost their lives.

George's life was indeed different in that he learned that his family moved to Michigan some fifty years ago. They migrated up from Mexico by way of

Bridges of Three Rivers

Arkansas, where his dad's grandparents worked in the fields of LA (Lower Arkansas). Then wanting to blend in more with this new country, they decided to move further north, and there was some seasonal work of picking apples in the Midwest.

George didn't know his daddy very well, because he died while serving as a marine in Vietnam during the Tet offensive of 1968, leaving his mother alone to take care of him, and his younger brother. Luckily his grandparents were there, for they moved to their farm to live, and to work. Their grandfather was a wise man; he taught George and Peter a lot about farming.

Now in their forties and with their children settled. These two doctors decided to give back to the community. Joining this group called *Doctors without Borders* seemed like the best thing to do. Not that it was easy, but the feeling of helping people far outweighed the risks.

Half of this story started when George decided that he wanted to become a doctor. The funny part was when he was fourteen he watched a television show that had a doctor named Kelly Bracket. The show was called Emergency, and although he thought the paramedics were cool, he realized that being a doctor was the bomb. His mom laughed when he told her that he wanted to be a doctor one day. She put her arms around him and said she was sorry to have laughed.

He didn't understand why she had laughed, so he asked her, and she told him that his grades needed to be better to be accepted into a medical college. "Oh now I understand," he said. From that day forward all he could think about was one day being a doctor. In school, his grades went up because he found the classes to be more interesting, even though he took harder courses like chemistry and microbiology.

After graduating then receiving some scholarships for medical colleges, he decided to join the Air Force and take advantage of their college programs. Once he agreed to talk to the recruiter about what job he could do, the one that impressed him most was pararescue. They were part of the Air Force Special Forces, and their job was to rescue downed pilots or any other member trapped behind enemy lines.

Training started in the San Antonio, TX area where he learned how to be an airman. When it came to the outdoor things George excelled. He even became an expert in his rifle qualification. Graduation was awesome! He was able to purchase plane tickets for his mom, little brother, and grandma, but his grandpa died a few years before when George was a freshman in high school.

He was trained in parachuting, scuba diving, advanced medical, and free fall. There were many other things he learned how to do, but other than one mission that he went on, he never had to use much of what he had learned because there was no war. Four years went by quickly. While he was there, he attended college in his spare time; enough to earn a two-year degree in biology. Shortly after returning home he decided to attend college at Notre Dame.

Life for her, Miss Shelia Ursula McCormick was well planned out. It was planned out, just not by her, and this is where the problem lay. Her daddy was steadfast that she would go to business school and take over the family company one day. On the other hand, Shelia's problem was that being a business owner and a doctor at the same time just wasn't in the cards.

She graduated from High school, and her grades were exceptionally high. A grade point average of 3.98 wasn't anything to be ashamed of. Her mom was on her dad's side in that she wanted her to stay in New York, and attend the local city college. Her dad was now semi-retired and was at home more often, so stress was starting to show on Shelia until one day a friend, a very good friend was talking more about how she was accepted into Notre Dame's political science program. Her friend kept talking as if the universe was trying to get her attention. Then it happened, she said "Eureka" and quite loudly!

Her friend stopped talking about Notre Dame and said "what?"

That's when Shelia proceeded to tell her about an acceptance letter that she had received from Notre Dame a week or two before. Her friend was now so excited that she quickly asked Shelia to accept the invitation. While thinking about all the pressure from home about running the business, she said: "yes, I want to go." There you have it; both Shelia and George would be attending medical school at Notre Dame.

CHAPTER 2

For the last 24 plus months they had been in the remotest part of the African desert. When they arrived, they didn't know what they were in for. At first, the desperate conditions took a toll on them. He had some experience in the Air Force, but that was many years ago, and he hadn't even gone camping since he was a young man. Although it's a funny thing how when you learn something under stress, you tend to store that information for when it's needed.

She didn't complain, she knew how much this meant to him, and that he convinced her that it would be worth the pain. The thought of this would bring on a laugh inside, but it never went any further. The problem wasn't the long working hours they were used to that as surgeons. What got them tired was the menial tasks that they would need to perform, at least until some of the indigenous people would arrive in the camp. I mean they hadn't even washed clothes or cooked much for many years. They were just too busy with their careers!

One thing for sure George used his military training that day to help stop those marauders from killing them. After a long restful sleep, they were reflecting on the previous day's adventure. He thought of the one mission he went on as a PJ (Para rescue) and how similarly stressful it was.

It started with a long flight from Andrews Air Force base to London, England which gave George and his team some needed time to rest. He had just finished some finals and was ready for a break. Spending a few hours in England practicing for their mission, they were now prepared to go, and evacuate their downed pilots. It was very dark when they loaded into this small Learjet for the mission. The flight would be around forty-five minutes, and he was very nervous. To train is one thing, but to go on a real mission brings it all into focus.

Over ten thousand feet, this was a HALO mission, which stands for; high altitude, with a low opening. They would have an oxygen tank, fly their bodies into an area close to the downed pilot, but not open their parachutes before 5,000 feet. There were only three PJ's going on this mission, they would all perform their specific jobs, and that was to give the downed pilots medical help, nourishment, and then bring them home. They were well qualified to fight off their enemy If they needed to do so.

Bridges of Three Rivers

This mission was classified so George could not share too much of the information. Let's say they jumped in, located the crashed plane, and then secured the pilots; but not without having to fend off a squad of enemy combatants. He remembers those few days very well and to this day he and his comrades still received presents from those pilot's every anniversary of that day they came home.

That afternoon her time was first spent listening to George, tell this story to her, and their companions. Telling stories wasn't something he did that often, but when he did they were amazing, or they made you think. This one was amazing and caused you to appreciate the people that go into the service of their country. Other than that she mostly kept to herself and thought about their children back home.

Luckily by now they had someone to attend to their needs and right now that was much appreciated! Her name was Shantel, when she arrived at the camp for the first time, she was poorly dressed, and very thin. Both George and Shelia had shown much compassion for her where they practically took care of her for the first couple of weeks. After that, she was in full strength, and they couldn't have found a better person to care for them than Shantel. George and Shelia are both extraordinary people.

Bridges of Three Rivers

In the village, they were taking care of the sick, just like they had been for almost two years. The funds for Doctors without Borders were becoming scarce, even with the doctors there pitching in all they could afford. Money has always been tight for these missions because of the medical supplies that they required. Sometimes these doctors would return to their home country and go on fundraising drives. Many high ranking business people, politicians, and celebrities would go above and beyond to support them.

When they first landed almost three years back, George immediately started organizing the hospital equipment, while Shelia worked on recruiting a critically needed surgery staff. This area was new to this type of relief, and thankfully some ex-military personnel volunteered to accompany the doctors over there. Some of the ex-military men were from the infantry, cooks, medical, and most importantly the engineers!

George liked working with the engineers; they all seemed to have a very can-do attitude. Anything that needed to be built or designed and these engineers were right there to assist. One instance he remembered was early on when the water supply was very inconsistent. There was water several miles away in the mountains, but the drive was hard with no roads, and dangerous because of the marauders. Taking a page from the Roman Empire, these engineers came up with a plan.

In the dark of the night, they would work with their night vision glasses on. The trick was to find where the closest underground water stream was and track it. They thought about drilling a borehole for water, but it would be so deep and costly. So instead, they would have to fight off the Marauders to get their water. Within a few weeks there was water flowing into the camp freely and hidden.

On Friday nights they decided to make it their dance party night. One of the couples there who were fans of Dancing with the Stars organized this. The first thing was to teach others how to dance. George and Shelia had taken lessons and went out at least once a month. Sometimes the dance night would be so competitive that they and the couple that started it would act as the judges.

There were no cell phones in use except one with a powered amplifier that would be turned on once or twice a week for phone calls. Shelia would always look forward to calling home to talk with her parents and children. One of her friends would tell her about the time her son was in Iraq, and he would call them on his cell phone. She would tell Shelia that it was bad enough him being over there, and that one time he told her that he was in the back of a truck monitoring a computer, and if he were hit with an artillery round he wouldn't even know it.

They never left to come home during their hitch and even started to learn some of the languages over there. The children were just as sweet as anywhere else. George used to think, *how can people hate others just because they don't look, speak, or act like them? People are just people no matter where you go.*

During their time they had other close calls with the marauders. At one time the town was surrounded and all their supplies were cut off for two weeks. Until some reinforcements arrived to bring the siege to an end. It was in the winter and it was a fortunate thing that they had just been resupplied. The snow was heavy in the mountains and the temperatures were freezing all around.

Surrounded they were trapped and with no way out to get water. The Marauders' intent was on plundering and killing all the people in the town. George met with the military leaders and formalized a plan to hold them off until the planes would arrive there within a week! The plan that was put together was to minimize the use of their arms and to set up trip wires where ever possible. George even shared some of the chemical supplies to make some bombs to help bolster their lot of Molotov cocktails.

The enemy would drive their vehicles towards the camp in reckless abandon. The military people inside the camp were puzzled as to why their enemy seemed to have no sense of what they were doing. The problem was, they had no education, and when the group offered to teach them they refused. Some were intimidated into this from the gang leaders. One thing for sure was; in a desolate place, all means of possessions were coveted.

Because the enemy vehicles would charge toward the camp, the engineers dug traps for the wheels to either get stuck in or go flat. This caused the rest to turn around and retreat. They didn't even return to get their wounded or injured. Day two soon approached with more snow and crazy vehicles trying to storm the gate.

During the night when the adversaries retreated to their encampment, the doctors went out with the others to bring in the wounded enemy. Some needed to be restrained while the doctors took care of their wounds. Day after day the same thing would happen, more attacks, and more dead or wounded. Talk about the definition of insanity, doing the same thing over and over again and expecting a different result.

Well, the people were holding out okay but the ammo was starting to get low, and the people were getting tired of the rations. On the seventh day, the air Calvary arrived and none too soon! Three helicopters flew in, and they were armed! Quickly, the marauders left their positions and returned to the mountain area.

A few months went by, then George's and Shelia's departure day drew near. They weren't sure if leaving was what they wanted, but there were a lot of changes during these two years away from home. All that was needed was for their replacements to arrive in ten days, then they would board the same plane, and leave.

During the final dance party, there were many sad faces especially from the indigenous people who had become fond of these two fine American doctors. This night was exceptional for them, for some reason that couldn't be explained, they just felt young again. George put his arm around Sheila while walking in the moonlight and said: "you are my girl."

This saying was some of the first words he had said to her when they first met many years back. The feelings he had for her were those of love, admiration, and family. Shelia could only feel these fantastic vibrations coming from him, then bombarding through to her heart and soul. She would only return them in the same intensity that he sent them to her. Just as all laws in the universe can't be broken. The law of reciprocity was indeed at play here.

Walking by the lake and looking up at the stars in this beautiful desert sky. Both were in love now more than ever and that night was magical. Smelling the cool fall night air, he would breathe in and remember all the times they had spent together here over the last two years. With her arm around his waist, she put her head on his shoulder, and thought of how lucky she was to have met him. Knowing that they were leaving the following day brought tears, but when they discussed the sadness, they both came to an agreement that their time spent helping others was so well worth it.

On waking up, she turned over to him, and kissed the back of his neck. Turning around to face her he smiled and said: "you were great last night."

This only made her blush and say "let's eat, I'm starving!"

Packed up and ready to go to the airport. The Airport was a bit of a stretch; let's say landing strip that is guarded by the local police. Looking over the horizon they spotted the plane, looks like a Cessna 210 or something, he thought. Well, he was almost right it was a 209 and held six people with little gear. Both of them decided to leave most of that behind to their friends.

Hitting the ground with a cloud of dust, and tracking down the runway, this little plane came to a halt. The Jeep then drove up with George in the back and Shelia in the passenger's seat. They exchanged greetings with the two new male doctors. One was from Alabama and the other one from California. The one from Alabama was recruited after his retirement and another one from Californian after serving in the army as a doctor.

While in the plane, they waved goodbye to the driver and the new doctors. Not looking out the window anymore, they then smiled a sheepish smile at each other, and the plane took off.

CHAPTER 3

When she left home to go to Notre Dame her parents had no idea what her plans were. That was their way of thinking since their little girl was a perfect student. Although she had chosen to go to medical school, it was against her dad's wishes, because he wanted her to get an MBA. However, she made one exception for him, and that was to minor in business.

It was vital for her to join the right seniority house so she picked Phi Alpha Beta Kappa. They were a mildly controlled house with just a few parties because their mission was to become the top students in their classes. This suited her well and her friends also held the same view.

Since she never had time for boys in high school, Shelia spent most of her teenage years studying, and helping out at the hospital. That is when she wasn't going to those boring business meetings with her dad. Her dad didn't believe that she wanted to become a doctor anyway.

She found college life to be different, even though studying to become a doctor wasn't easy; it was easier than high school. For being away from home, she was left with some free time after completing her school work. Her freshman year was very easy, too easy for her, and now that it was over, she decided to loosen up a bit, and enjoy her youth.

The summers were what got her dander up! First was coming home and being bombarded by her dad about business school, and him not even thinking about her major being in medical. She would shake her head afterward and say *doesn't he understand that I am going to be a doctor one day?* For some reason, he couldn't believe that, so the summer was spent pleasing her daddy who loved her so much, but couldn't see how talented she was at medicine. His little girl was talented at anything she tried to do.

One of the hospitals in the area was an inspiration for her when she was growing up. She remembers a time when her mom was sick and they thought she wouldn't make it. Meeting the nurses and the doctors was something that struck a lasting chord with Shelia. Watching them work and seeing the respect the doctors had for their patients was so different than her dad's business world.

One of the young doctors was handsome and had a very good wit. She would often go to work there during the summer in the hope of spending some time with DR. Steel MD. She couldn't wait to return to the hospital hoping to see him again. Dr. Steel had gotten married while Shelia was in college, so she realized that he would be a very good friend and a colleague one day.

"MY Sophomore year at Notre Dame begins now and I'm ready!" she said to herself. This year was going to be different. No more Miss-boring-rich-girl from New York, no more of that for this girl was ready to meet boys, and party! All Her friends returned except for one, Miss Janet who graduated, and started her internship back home in Alabama.

Growing up most little girls liked My Little Pony. The girls at the seniority house were no different, so they thought of their friendship as the ponies. Shelia didn't pick her pony, but because of her wealth, her friends wanted her to be Rarity. Sometimes when they wanted to warn each other, they would use those pony names. Twilight was the leader; she was the most grounded of the five, Apple Jack was new because Janet graduated and left.

Shelia started to look around the campus at the young men going to medical school. But she didn't limit her search to just medical majors only. There were some who were studying engineering, law, and a few even in business. Business majors were very different from what she was looking for. She would share the names of the men that were somewhat suitable to her with her friends.

Twilight would agree with some, but Pinky Pie felt that she was using her mind too much, and not her heart. Then Apple Jack, who was new didn't know Rarity that well, but noticed that the list went from one extreme to another. Rainbow Dash and Flutter Shy weren't ready to give their opinions just yet.

While talking with Twilight, she asked her what she thought about their opinions. Twilight was a very wise pony girl and told her that she should use her mind to make the decisions that only came from her heart. Thinking this over, she could just say that she would do her best. No those weren't her final words but, they sure could come back to bite her.

Party, party, party that is the direction she had chosen to meet men. Tonight she managed to convince her pony friend Rainbow Dash and Pinky Pie to accompany her. This wasn't a big party, but a couple of the men's seniority houses put it together. The theme was *Animal House*. Drinking and smoking are synonymous with college parties and this movie.

Shelia was not prepared for this having never drunk anything outside of dinner wine before. They were moving around like wolves in a pin full of cattle. Only Pinky Pie had done any amount of drinking before, but tonight she seemed to forget to warn the other girls about the pitfalls it brings. Kegs of beer were rolled out, the music was loud, and there were snacks everywhere! What more could you ask for, Shelia thought *this will be fun.*

Meeting men was on her agenda and she drank some beer when they had begged her to. However, she didn't like the taste that much and that meant she wasn't eager to drink any on her own. She met a few nice young men and gave them her contact information. Rainbow Dash was getting too drunk, so Rarity and Pinky Pie went into action to get her back home before she got into trouble!

Hangover! That was the word for this day, and luckily it was Saturday! Shelia woke up with the worst headache she could ever remember. Knocking on the door was Twilight, she had already checked on Pinky Pie and Rainbow Dash, where she brought her some aspirins, and a big glass of seltzer water. Now it was Rarity's turn to receive some Dr. Twilight medical treatment.

Lessons learned? Well not yet, Shelia still wanted to pursue the party angle. Two of the boys contacted her and she was going on a date with one tonight. His name was Brian, he was from Chicago, he went home on the weekends for his mom's cooking, and to have his clothes washed. *How nice* Shelia thought.

He arrived a few minutes early, so Flutter Shy opened the door. She let him in and had him sit on the sofa where he would wait for Shelia to come down. Not too sure where he would take her. She decided to dress a little bit casual, wearing a blue blouse, a pair of her blue jeans, and some brown sandals. He was dressed like most guys at school, jeans and a polo shirt with sneakers. So off they went in his jet black 1998 Monte Carlo.

"Have you been here before?" Brian asked as they pulled into a local Bennigan's.

"No, not here, we usually go to Leonardo's Pizza."

They spent the evening talking mostly about school. He also was studying to be a doctor and looked forward to working in the Chicago area. She liked him as a friendly young man but wasn't sure if there was any spark. Although he thought he liked her, he didn't seem to feel the same vibe from her. All is well that ends well, she didn't offer her lips for a goodnight kiss, and he didn't call her again.

After returning home from class, her pony friends called her, and all asked about her date. The night before, she came home and went straight to her room without talking to anyone. Twilight asked if Brian had treated her well and she told her that he was a perfect gentleman. Rainbow Dash then asked if they were going out on another date. Shelia told her no, and that there wasn't any magic there. The others thought about that, and two of them seemed to think maybe they could pursue him.

The pursuit went on and on, party after party, and some close calls. Shelia was putting too much energy into finding a man and not concentrating on school. At one party, she got too drunk, and one of the young men tried to have his way with her. If not for Twilight being there he might have succeeded!

Some of the girls that would go out with her noticed that getting drunk wasn't exclusive to becoming a medical doctor. So that night she was going alone until for the first time Twilight decided not to allow that to happen. Going with her and trying not to "get in the way or be a party pooper." She managed to drink some, dance around talking with the boys, but all the while Twilight had no intentions of doing anything with these young men.

She looked around to start the wind down to go home, it was nine-thirty, and Twilight had lost the whereabouts of one Rarity Sparkle. Then she walked into the kitchen telling one boy to step aside; she doesn't have time for him. Then she noticed the stairs to the second floor. She thought *oh no, she can't be up there!* She went knocking on the doors until she heard a voice say "Twilight is that you?"

Fortunately the door was left unlocked, so she barged-in, and quickly ran to the bed grabbing her friend by the hand, and rushing her out of the room. The guy was so drunk that he couldn't react in time. While leaving, running down the stairs, all she could hear was him say "hey babe, where are you going?"

They went out the door and into the car; this seemed like an armed getaway from a movie. Back to the house, Twilight ran inside and requested Rainbow Dash to come out and help bring Rarity in. Twilight wasn't very pleased with these parties that Rarity would go to, and as soon as she was sober, she would hear it from her.

Report cards came out, and her daddy wasn't pleased, and her mom was disappointed, but didn't want to "pile on." All she could say was that she was sorry and she had learned her lesson. The thought of not graduating because of her daddy withdrawing his financial support of paying her school fees wasn't what she wanted to contemplate at all.

The giant step in rebuilding their friendship was when she asked for Twilight's help. Because just like the Little Pony's, friendship is the most important thing. She was back on track in school and started getting good grades again. Looking for a boyfriend was still on her agenda, but this time around, she would use her mind in service to her heart. Not sure how all this would work, she understood from some of her psyche classes that these two need to work together. Right there Shelia thought that she would follow her heart and confirm the feelings with her friend Twilight; at least until she could get her brain onboard.

Two years later Shelia would graduate, meet lots of young men, go on numerous dates, but never really found her true love. But at least she was not in college. Her parents were so proud of her. Her dad and mom would both shed tears of joy watching her earn her first degree. Then she would go for her internship to become a medical doctor and who knows maybe meet the love of her life?

CHAPTER 4

The weather was cold. It was one of the coldest winters in years. Life on the farm wasn't easy, if it were, more people would do farming. That's what George would hear at the local feed store when he would be with his mom. She was a strong-willed woman who took over after his dad died in the war. Their wedding anniversary day would always make her sad and George couldn't understand why she kept crying for him. He didn't know him that well because he was shipped to Vietnam when George was only two years old.

Work was never done until dinner time, and even then there were the dishes to clean. Now that he had set his sights on going to medical school those grades needed to be perfect. He was a smart teenager, never getting involved in the high school things that would prevent him from getting good grades. He didn't even have a girlfriend, but there were a few that he liked to spend time with, mostly to study for exams. He quickly learned that girls seemed to be either smarter than most boys or at least better disciplined.

His high school years brought a lot of changes for him. One of the most important was that he was now older, bigger, and able to do more things around the farm. His mom didn't work, and his grandparents were retired and living off their social security checks. At least the small farm was paid for. Unfortunately, his mom didn't grow up on a farm, so the in-laws taught her all they could. It was their only means of survival, but it produced enough, even though they only had little to put into it.

When George entered his senior year, he was six-one, 195 pounds, and he was very strong. During physical education class one day the coach noticed something special about him. They were playing football and for the first time George was playing quarterback. They had played for ten or fifteen minutes, and he had got a feel for throwing the ball. This happened when coach Bell was walking over to tell them to start winding up the game.

Their game was all tied up, then, one of the boys that would line up on the outside slot as a wideout told George that the coach was coming. He looked over to where the coach was walking and then looked back at his wideout and said what do you want to do? The young man told him that he was getting open deep on the post route on a specific play. They both agreed that since the coach was coming to tell them to quit, they might as well try one deep play.

His teammates all said "what it's at least 60 yards to the goal line, maybe further!" George thought *why not try it* and called the play. They all lined up, and he looked over the defense and noticed that they were pretty much in the same formation as before. There where no deep safeties and the cornerbacks weren't too far off the line. Under center he said "hut-one, hut-two, red, red hike." With the ball in his hands, he took a deep seven-step drop, looked at the inside of the field where the middle linebacker was doing a read, and waiting for the tight end to come across.

Coach Bell stopped to watch the play. He noticed the tight end making his cut to the inside. He looked carefully seeing if George could get the ball to him, and then watched as he did a hard pump fake in that direction. The coach was almost frozen when he didn't see the ball come out and hit the tight end in the bread basket. Instead he looked back at George and noticed that his arm was fully extended forward without the ball. Quickly looking up he spotted the most perfect spiral throw of a football he had ever seen in high school. His wideout was speeding down the field with the safety backpedaling as quickly as he possible could.

Then the wideout made a sharp cut around the fifteen-yard line to inside the right post of the end zone.

Bam! The ball dropped into his arms around the two-yard line, and he just ran in untouched!

All coach Bell could say was, damn! He stood there with his jaw hanging down and calculated that George just threw a perfect corner post pass some 63 yards. He begged, pleaded with him to join the team. They were three and three, but with four games left they could make the playoffs. He joined the team during his senior year, and they made the playoffs, but lost in the regional tournament.

He thought about going to one of the local colleges while spending the summer on the farm, but he didn't want to leave his mom, and brother to work the farm. He knew his dad was in the marines and for some reason he wanted to do the same. His mom tried to talk him out of it, but financially it made a lot of sense. Fortunately, they were not in any war, so his chances of dying were not high. I know that's a morbid way of looking at things, but it made sense. Also when he enlisted, he made one big choice, which was to join the Air Force, and this made his mom happy.

He left home to fly to San Antonio, Texas for basic training. During his first days of processing, he did some significant things. One was to take out a large allotment to go directly into his mom's bank account. The other was to sign up for the college deductions which would be enough for his college education until he was through. It was a lot of fun, not hard at all physically but mentally he learned a lot of cool things about the Air Force. After graduating, he didn't go very far for his medical training.

In the Air Force medical training he had to learn a lot about battlefield treatments. He would think some of these treatments were very much like the show Emergency that he watched on TV when growing up. After medical school he went to an army school in Georgia where he learned how to parachute. He would be there for three weeks, then a two week break to go home, and spend time with his family. While at home he did a lot of farm work which he missed a little bit. Then when the two weeks were over he flew down to the beautiful keys of Florida to learn scuba diving.

The four years in the Air Force weren't too uneventful. During this time he went on one rescue mission and earned a two-year degree in biology. Knowing the last day was coming soon, George made sure he spent every waking minute with his friends. He didn't want to lose contact with his PJ team. Thus he wrote down all their contact information.

His mother was so happy to see him back home again. Later on, she told him how much the money she received every month helped her tremendously. This made George feel great, because he felt guilty about leaving her and his younger brother alone. Laughing at him feeling guilty, she said how proud she was of him, and that he had nothing to feel guilty about.

Since his brother was graduating from high school and probably going off to college or who knew where, the family decided it was time to sell the farm, and move closer to town. It didn't take too long to sell, and they paid cash for a home, with some money still left in the bank.

George applied for medical school at Notre Dame where he would only need to do a little over two years to graduate into medical school. He went off to school which was less than 50 miles from home! *This was perfect* he thought. Coming home every weekend and always being close if needed.

Going to medical school was George's dream for many years and now that day had arrived. While sitting in the register's office, his mind started to wonder. His main thoughts were about when he was young and how he would visualize the day he would be attending Notre Dame. These visions felt so real that he even wondered if his mind wasn't somehow responsible for making this happen.

The first day in college was a very powerful beginning to his ability to create his new life. There were some books he had read about the metaphysical parts of your consciousness. These books helped him to become a person that didn't allow the outside world to affect his inner self.

He was curious about his one year of playing high school football so he tried out for the team.

Quickly he found out that there were plenty of good quarterbacks on the team. Not knowing the play calls and overall language of football, he decided that his heart was just not into it enough. However, while there he joined the same intramural sports, like tennis and golf.

All the things that were to be done had been done, or they came second to his desire to become a doctor. Many of his teachers had an appreciation for the work he had done while in the Air Force. Some would ask him questions or listen to his stories, especially about the one rescue mission he went on. Friendly was the word he would use to describe his opinion of his classmates.

George attended a few parties in his two-plus years at Notre Dame. The one enjoyment he got was going to watch their Irish play football. The more he attended, the more he thought about trying out for the team. Talking to his mom about this, she didn't feel it was a wise way of utilizing his time. After all, she would remind him about how much time he was already spending in study hall to make good grades.

Early in his years of college he set his sights on all the local hospitals in his hometown area where he would go to do his internship. Knowing that he would have to wait for an opening, he made sure to keep in touch with them. Internships are not a dime a dozen, they can be very hard to get, and the doctors are very selective as to who they bring in to mentor.

His little brother was doing well in high school and his mom's health had improved. Moving from the farm brought many sad thoughts, but it was for the better. His mom was getting tired of working to keep it running. However, she found a job in town at a local nursery. This was a perfect fit because there was so much she learned on the farm about maintaining plants. His brother Peter was also free since he was not playing sports, therefore he had more time to do his homework, and he had a part-time job stocking groceries.

He wanted to graduate with honors, but fell short by two-tenths of a point, with an average of 3.48. George met a couple of girls in college that he would date. However, none of them seemed to be what he was searching for in a long term relationship. There was one girl named Shelia that he noticed but thought she was just too wild for him.

Finally, he graduated and was now off to perform his internship at a hospital near his hometown of Three Rivers, Michigan. This couldn't have made him happier. To help his mom out, he moved into her home near the city, and helped his brother out in college.

CHAPTER 5

Six to eight years, that's what they told her, when she showed up at the hospital. Shelia didn't mind this internship, for it was far away from New York, and her dad's business world.

Where is she? She got her second choice of Seattle, Washington. Her first choice was Hawaii. Thus, that was a pipe dream if ever there was one. The hospital was nice, on the south side of town. The doctor that chose to bring her in was a very calm and confident man. He didn't let things disturb him and was always ready for a challenge. I suppose that's why he chose Shelia.

"Dr. Morgan, it's so nice to meet you, my name is Shelia McCormick."

He looked at her and smiled, then said "welcome, we've been waiting for you." Then he rolled his eyes like a vampire.

This introduction broke the ice. Dr. Morgan was in his late fifties and was a big fan of the old monster movies. All the nurses would be on their toes during the Halloween season because he would try to scare them whenever possible. She was happy to be in an environment where people had a good sense of humor.

They were both laughing in his office on her first day. Dr. Morgan wanted to sit her down and explain their routines, now that all the books and pamphlets were handed out. He then started asking her some questions about who she was. Once she started talking, he couldn't help but find some of her college stories to be funny, and then he shared some of his own. They seemed to have several things in common like parents that wanted them to do something else.

Getting a place would not be too easy, until she met one of the nurses there, whose name was Susan. She had just recently divorced with a four-year-old daughter. She owned a three bedroomed home, so she offered one of them to Shelia for a ridiculously low price! Shelia quickly accepted because she didn't want her parents to be supporting her constantly.

Life in Seattle is great, she said to herself. And when her parents would write or call she always told them how great she was doing. Her mom would start to press her on whether she had met any men. Her mom wanted grandchildren. Plus she thought if Shelia was to get married and have children then she would have an excuse to move out there.

After four years Shelia was doing great, her friend Susan sort of adopted her as her little sister, and Susan's daughter Lilly called her aunt Shelia. Susan never thought of herself as a matchmaker, but once she started dating again, she knew that Shelia would need to move on. Shortly thereafter Susan met someone named Brad. And she knew that he was the one she wanted to marry. They set a date for ten months to tie the knot.

Very delicately Susan started to introduce Shelia to some of her male friends of her fiancé and hoping that one of them would be mister right. She did this very slowly, and most of the times she would use an excuse of either going on a double date or just meeting these men at sporting events. Shelia was so engaged with all the beauty that was happening around her that she didn't have any idea what Susan was doing.

Susan's wedding was beautiful. Her new husband was a very successful man in the arts. Their wedding took place on Port Susan on board a huge yacht. There were lots of people dancing and playing games that day. Susan invited most of the hospital crew that she worked with over the years.

One of Brad's best men whose name was Jacob asked Shelia for a dance. On the dance floor, she looked into his eyes, and couldn't help but notice how blue they were. He had a lot of charm. This night he was in the zone dancing the foxtrot with her, leading the way like a well-taught dancer, and that left her impressed with his style. His tux fit him like a glove, for this one was tailored by only the best. Not very tall, he was a few inches under six feet, but well built, probably from hiking, and swimming. Sitting with her at his table, this just all seemed to be planned. They talked and danced the rest of the night. Jacob would say funny things to her so well, that they showed his depth of brevity.

Mission accomplished for Susan, Brad, and Shelia's mom. Jacob and Shelia dated for a few months before he asked for her hand in marriage. With only one year left of residency, she was ready to settle down. They were deeply in love, both moving to Seattle from the east. He was from the Philadelphia, Pennsylvania area and you know Shelia was from New York City. Brad offered his yacht for their wedding, and it was beautiful. Her dad was very handsome walking her down the aisle. Shelia's dad would also spend some time later on with Brad talking about his business. "Dad was always working," Shelia told her new husband Jake, short for Jacob.

They bought a nice little home just outside of Redmond. Shelia became a doctor and after a few years joined a practice in Redmond close to home. Jake continued working for Brad and also did a small business with her dad too. Over time, they had a boy and a girl, named Steven and Julie. Raising two children, being married, and being a doctor. Her life was good, but at the same time she was too preoccupied. Three years into their marriage Jake started spending a lot of time in New York with her dad.

In New York City, Jake thought that this is where he needed to be. Since Shelia had no intentions of running her dad's business, then Jake could only think that it should go to him. This started to disturb her, especially when he would be gone for weeks at a time, and leaving her to take care of the children, and their home. Somehow she always knew that her dad would find a way to get her involved in the business.

Calling Jake home wasn't something she felt right about, but this was getting ridiculous. "Jake this has to stop, what do you think you are doing being gone for so long?"

"I'm only trying to help you keep what's rightfully yours. Don't you want the children to have your daddy's business one day?"

This was hard to argue with but she felt that he was going about it all wrong. As the conversation grew, Jake started to realize that he wasn't the main breadwinner in his home, and this disturbed him. It didn't take long before Shelia hired a private investigator to find out what Mr. Jake was doing and it wasn't good. He was trying to use his position being married to Shelia to have important documents signed exclusively over to him. This would give him over fifty percent ownership of her daddy's companies.

She moved quickly to divorce him, and when it was finalized, she would never see him again. She assumed that he went back to Philadelphia. Neither Brad nor Susan wanted anything to do with him either.

Living at home would only bring George closer to the truth of his feelings about family. Hearing the stories his mom and grandparents told him about how much his dad looked forward to coming home. This made George want to continue in that vein of getting married and having a family. He made his desires known to the universe so much that he even wrote them down!

My intentions are to one day meet and marry the love of my life. Become a successful doctor and later be the head surgeon of Three Rivers Community Hospital. On October 12, 1992, my wife will give birth to our first child. My preference would be to have a boy, and we will name him after my father, Juan Martin Esperanza. In two years, on March 3, 1994 we will have our second child, a beautiful girl and her mom will choose her name. Our life together will be full of joy, excitement, and we will be together beyond our fiftieth anniversary.

George believed in his dreams, and that day he put his best foot forward. The first day at the hospital, he was ready to start his residency, and he was chosen by an ex-Air Force doctor who had made it to Lt. Colonel shortly before she retired. She was a very pleasant looking lady only five-two, with auburn hair, and gorgeous green eyes. He could only imagine what a knock-out she must have been not too many years ago.

Seeing George standing there she made the first move. "Hello, you must be Staff Sargent George Esperanza?"

Tongue tied he didn't think he was able to speak. "Why? Yes, that's my name, I was that rank in the Air Force. You are Dr. Fitzpatrick correct?"

Some unintended and some intended silence from them both followed. Dr. Rebecca Fitzpatrick had to laugh because of how shy he seemed to be. She then said, "for goodness sake George you were a PJ, so don't be shy, you have a lot to be proud of."

Now with that uncomfortableness out of the way, she proceeded to welcome him to his new life as a future doctor. After talking for a few hours in her office about his life, then doing her homework on him, and knowing some of the pilots that were rescued. These pilots who were brought to the hospital for her care left her with a very high held honor for the men that rescued them. Being a Christian by faith, she always thought of how they would risk their lives to save others.

This made George feel so good, and after learning about her service, he felt so honored to have been chosen by her. They decided to break for lunch, and he learned that Dr. Fitz was what she was always called for short. Down the stairs, they went to the staff lounge and cafe'. *What a first day,* he thought while sitting next to his mentor. They finished their lunch, and

Dr. Fitz was ready to introduce him to the rest of the staff.

With a meeting already on the schedule, Dr. Fitz made sure her staff would stay twenty minutes after their shift. There were only two people who couldn't stay late. Both had children in school, and one had to leave an hour earlier. George was introduced to his new colleagues, and Dr. Fritz made sure he didn't leave out his time in the Air Force. At least three of the nurses were happy to see a new young doctor who wasn't married, even the married ones too.

CHAPTER 6

Common interests, time spent together, and then all the other intangibles add up. Helping one of the doctors today was something he looked forward to doing. One of the most exciting things they did on day two was to examine a twelve-year-old who fell off his bike. George liked doing the full examination and thought that none of it was a waste of time, especially after watching the doctors in the Air Force when they would bring their rescued pilots in.

There were some problems during his first couple of years, but there was nothing he couldn't handle. There was a time when dating one of the nurses led to a minor altercation. This was their third date, and she wanted to take him somewhere that she used to hang out. Yes, this was a mistake, but it all worked itself out. A former boyfriend of her was feeling a little too brave and too much beer will do that to you.

This man thought that she would go home with him tonight and his mind was thinking back to when they dated a couple of times. She quickly dumped him when George showed up at the hospital. This would leave her available to date him, and as you can see that she finally did. He grabbed her arm then told her she was going home with him. That's when George used some aikido on him that he learned in the military. When Dr. Fitz heard about how he handled this, she was impressed, but he didn't think it was a big deal.

George dated three of the nurses over a period of three years and two women that he met through his family. There was this lovely girl named Christa who he noticed was different from the others in a lot of ways. He thought of her as an enigma for she did not give in to the pressures of what other people thought especially about the things that were of fashion, trends or just being cool. George could always talk with her about the things that he felt were positive and were in his future imagined life.

Dating Christa was something he looked forward to every Friday night. This worked out very well because during the week George never knew what time he would leave the office. Since he was close to getting his residency over, he still felt obligated to give his best to his mentors. The most important one was Dr. Fritz, she earned his admiration.

Bridges of Three Rivers

Turning 30 in a month, George was not trying to think about his goals. He was told that the best thing to do was to write down your goals, or affirmations, and then leave them at that. In the back of his mind, he wrote down that by his 30th birthday he would be married. *Then comes this problem*, he said, although he wasn't a doctor yet, there wasn't a date set because he didn't know how long his residency would be.

Christa wasn't pushing him to propose to her, even though she wanted to marry him and settle down. They had talked about it, and she was ready to move to wherever his practice would be. That night, he just wanted to relax and spend the weekend with her. The summer was very hot, and the two days they would spend in Traverse City would be perfect. On stopping at Christa's place, parking the car, and then walking up the steps to the door, he said to himself, *yes she's going to be so happy tomorrow. She* opened the door and let him in. He tried his level best to hide the smile that was creeping up on his face.

"Okay, what's up," she said.

"Nothing, I'm just so happy to escape the heat."

I don't know if she believed his answer or not, but he didn't give her any idea of what he was doing. Their drive would be several hours long, so they left early. The first stopover was to eat dinner, and the plan was to stop for about an hour. George bought a Chevy Silverado a couple of years before because the old truck he had used from the farm days was now starting to break down

They talked about their future, mostly because that's where George wanted to start. He was bent on making sure they both wanted the same things. He had learned in the military how to interrogate people without causing any harm to them. There were times during the drive that he wondered if she wasn't saying what she thought he wanted to hear? Then doing some reflection he realized that most of her answers had to be genuine.

Pulling in for the night at the Grand Traverse City Hotel for sleep was undoubtedly on their quick agenda. They were so tired that he wasn't sure if he wouldn't have to carry her upstairs. In the room, they went and plopped right on the bed. No change of clothes, no nightcap, and they didn't even brush their teeth! Well, the two were so much in love that they would shower and take care of all that hygiene in the morning.

The sun was up, the coffee was delivered, and their breakfast ordered. They would take turns in the bathroom. Christa decided to shower first while he brushed his teeth. That day was to be a day of sailing on the Grand Traverse Bay. Eating breakfast and breathing in all the smells of coffee, roses, and scented candles.

It was time to go downstairs to get in the car. He made her feel rushed, so she suspected something was up, and she therefore asked while sitting in the car "why all the hurry, where are we going?"

"You'll see soon enough," he said smiling.

She accepted his answer even though he didn't answer her completely, but felt confident that he had a good plan for the day. The last time he came up here, he was very young, but it was all coming back to him. After parking the car, they walked up to the building on the dock.

Before they could get to the door, a tall older man with a captain's outfit walked out. This man asked them, "are you the Esperanza couple?" This caught her by surprise, and when she tried to answer her throat seemed to be as dry as the Arizona desert.

George laughed a little bit from that, then he held her hand, and answered him "yes, Captain we are."

"Well then follow me."

Tightening his hand, she said "Esperanza couple."

George then said, "one day dear, one day soon."

On the boat they were on with about thirty other people. She had talked with him about how much she wanted to go on a boat again one day. While growing up, her dad would take her out on his fishing boat. It wasn't very big, and they would mostly fish in the local lakes near their home.

The air that day was cool and moist, and that's all she could think about. While standing next to her on the port side, he wanted to say something and then suddenly thought *why mess up this perfect moment with words.*

Later, they both stood on the deck resting their bodies against the railing with their arms intertwined, and deep in thought. Soon the first mate came walking around asking if anyone wanted something to drink. They were a little thirsty, both ordered a bottle of mineral water, and looked at one another with a big smile. When the first mate walked away, they kissed. This kiss was one that George put his entire heart and soul into. So much so that she sensed something very powerful from it!

"What was that all about?" She asked him.

Trying to be coy he said "just a passionate kiss to the one woman I love more than any other."

Laughing she asked "are there others?"

George said "only one girl before I met you, but none since then."

They spent several hours there together and even had lunch on the yacht. Their lunch consisted of some light seafood with vegetables and some Chardonnay. The scenery was perfect, he told her about his plans for their evening. He told her that after the boat ride he wanted to take her dancing, then dinner, and a walk along the shoreline in the moonlight. *What a perfect man* she thought then wrapped her arms around him!

Getting off the boat, he jumped across the platform bridge between the boat, and the dock. He reached out his hand and escorted her across. Wow, she liked that a lot, he knew how to make her feel special. They entered the car and took off to the room to relax before they would go dancing. They talked about the boat ride while changing clothes and then rested on the bed.

Both were dressed to the hilt for a night of dancing. He knew how much she loved to dance, so much so that she was on the ballroom dance team in college. His work was certainly cut out for him, and he loved learning how to dance from her. Their limo that would be taking them to the ballroom had arrived, and this caught her by surprise as she wasn't aware of it.

Her dress was designed by one of the finest designers from Paris. Long in the back, but with a very tricky cut in the front, if you can imagine an oval shape cut just below the knees. It was an aquamarine colour that slowly turned to a bright white near the top. This transition began just above the hips and from there downwards was a solid aquamarine colour. The arms did the same transition around the elbows with the white going up of course. Around her neck was a three-inch collar that stood up but in the front, it tapered to nothing. Just around her breast was another oval cut only that it was horizontal, not vertical like the one below the knees.

She wore a beautiful gold chain of about eight gauge width with a magnificent light sapphire blue stone cut in sixteen shapes forming another vertical oval. Her hair wasn't done up in any Princess Grace style. Christa wanted to keep her hair the way she had whenever she dressed up before and nothing different. It was about shoulder length, dirty blonde, and very thick with long waves.

George was taken aback by just how gorgeous she looked that night. He rented a tux for this occasion and used his old Air Force patient leather shoes, he called them his low quarters, which was the common military term also. He opened a glass of champagne to toast in the evening and all the good things that were to come.

Before he planned all this, he spent some time with Dr. Fritz asking for her opinion on setting it up. First was to dance, so upon arrival, they dropped their stuff off at the table and hit the floor. The music was a slow one with some steady rhythm, so they decided to start with a foxtrot. Positioning his hand properly, she looked at him, smiled, and gave him a wink. Nervousness wasn't half of what he was going through because pleasing her on the dance floor meant so much to him.

Two hours later they were not only bushed, but they were starving. What was on their minds was having a glass of champagne in the limo, then a glass of wine with a pitcher of water, and solid food. While spending some time in Europe, George got a taste for fine French cuisine. There just happened to be a small restaurant by the boardwalk that specialized in French cuisine. She had never really had food prepared in this style of cooking before. When the limo pulled around to the front, they were then let out, and off they went.

At the door greeting them was the Maitre d, who asked them to follow him to their table. Christa was enjoying this because she had never been given this type of attention anywhere before. Looking over the menu, she wasn't sure what to order. George ordered something in French and she was turned on with this man's suaveness. Dinner was served but not before they had some bread, cheese, and a little taste of red wine.

The food was out of this world, so much so she joked with him about wanting to spend their honeymoon in Paris or at least somewhere in France. He just lifted his glass and said a toast to that. After dinner, he stood up and went to her side, gave her a gentle kiss on the neck, and then said "would you like to walk with me in the moonlight?"

"Of course," she said, and managed to answer him in her best and most classy way possible.

He then pulled her chair out while she stood up and turned to him. He then took her left hand, pulled her to him, and they walked out through the back door. Right outside, there was the boardwalk, and the smell of the night air by the bay. With their arms around each other, they were both breathing in the love they shared.

Shortly after leaving the restaurant, they entered the boardwalk, which turned and went out to the bay. They walked slowly, timing their steps with one another. Holding each other tight and enjoying the closeness the warmth brought.

On looking up they spotted a falling star, quickly she looked at him and said "make a wish, make a wish! I've always loved making wishes on falling stars."

He chuckled and said, "I did my dear."

There they were, at the end of the boardwalk, and with a falling star to have made a wish on. Who knows what she wished for, maybe the same thing he did? Anyway, tonight we shall see if any wishes will come true.

He moved his arm from around her waist then turned around to face her. Not sure what was happening she supposed he wanted to kiss her, so she leaned forward. Not to miss the moment he obliged and kissed her. Then he held both of her hands, took one step back and dropped to one knee. Tears were already starting to fall down her cheek. Dropping her right hand, he reached into his pocket, pulled out a tiny ring box.

He then said "Christa Anne Miller, will you marry me?"

Without hesitation, she said, "yes, Dr. George Fernando Esperanza."

They walked back to the limo. She stopped crying and told him that her wish just came true. He made a thinking man's pose and agreed that his too had come true. This night he asked her to marry him and his wish was for her to say yes. Life was certainly turning out the way he envisioned it many years before.

CHAPTER 7

Her life was right there in Redmond, Washington and that's where she would raise her children. Jake was not all a bust, he loved their children, helped her with them before he went crazy for money, and power. Little Steven would ask her where daddy was long before she divorced him. Her baby girl Julie was so sweet and mommy wasn't even going to mention Jake to her anytime soon.

This is not to say that Shelia was bitter, just that she didn't want her life or that of her children to be caught up in negativity. It didn't take long for Jake to become envious of her status as a doctor. Each week he insisted on doing the bills; they were quite apart in amounts when it came to their paychecks. Sometimes he would say something to her about how hard it was to be in sales with the way the economy was. She never considered things being bad, and the occupant of the Whitehouse didn't really hold any sway on her prosperity.

Leaving all that complaining and whining behind her for there was so much of life out there. That day was the first day of their first vacation together. Excited was just an understatement; Shelia was giddy. Traveling north up the coast to the Anacortes' Islands they were going on a boat ride to watch the orca whales. The kids were as excited as she was and when they pulled in, they were so jumpy.

The good thing was that Steven was old enough to help her with Julie; since she had just started walking, she never wanted to be held for long. Walking over to the sidewalk that led to the dock, there was a huge sign. The sign had a large painting of an orca whale. When Julie saw it, she yelled so loudly that even little Steven jumped, and screamed too. Taking a deep breath, Shelia couldn't help but be happy that her children would be excited to see the whales.

Before boarding the boat, she exchanged some pleasant words with the young man taking the tickets. Slowly shaking her head, she thought *now wasn't he a nice young man?* Not that she felt all men weren't nice, but after the debacle with Jake, she needed a positive example. At least that's what was required in this age, more men that were friendly. Her inner self said *would you stop thinking about him and all that you feel is wrong. Why not just relax, enjoy the day, and for God's sake love your children!*

Bridges of Three Rivers

"Mommy, when are we going to see the whales?" Little Julie asked as she tried to run to the side of the boat.

Quickly, Steven was dispatched to stop her, and then she screamed. This was not something he liked, but the good thing was that his mommy was right there to help him. Adults enjoyed the fresh air, especially out on a boat in northern Washington. Now as far as children are concerned, not so much, they only want excitement. Most of the people were okay with Julie's outburst, some mad ugly faces, and that bothered Shelia.

It wasn't until near noon that the Captain called out on the speaker that a couple of orcas were spotted about a quarter mile ahead of them. A loud cheer went up from the passengers. Steven looked at Julie and told her that soon they would see the whales. She put her hands together from the news, and her whole attitude changed to excitement.

Bring binoculars, why didn't I bring the binoculars? Oh well. The kids would probably have some trouble sharing them so it might have been a blessing. Too bad that wasn't what Shelia was thinking, so for the next twenty minutes she was stuck thinking how stupid she was for forgetting them. This was disturbing her until some people in the boat yelled "look, there they are!"

Julie jumped into mommy's arms so fast that she almost knocked her over. Steven was standing up on one of the deck chairs looking out. With the waves bouncing so high and the people moving back and forth it was hard to locate them. Then in unison, Steven and Julie screamed "there they are!"

Some jumped up out of the water, so the people all let out a loud ah sound. The weather was just perfect this day in the sound except for some mix-up of Shelia taking Julie to the bathroom with her when she didn't want to wait for her mommy in the stall. Other than that, Steven was the perfect little man. Seeing her children laugh having fun was so healing to her soul.

They had a stopover on the drive home in Marysville for burgers and milkshakes. Julie just loved strawberry milkshakes.

Her mom never considered living in the west, let alone the Pacific Northwest. Anyway, that was before her little girl got married and had for her two beautiful grandchildren. Shelia's mom convinced her dad to get a winter condo in Seattle. I say convinced to be polite, let's say if he didn't agree, well she would be in Seattle permanently, and with half of his empire. It's funny how careful most wealthy people are with protecting their money.

It was great having her mom come to visit. When he could make some time from work, her dad would come too, but that seemed to be less often. With

Shelia having a practice in Redmond now for over three years, the thought of her taking over the business was a moot point. This pleased Shelia and her mom very much, so all's good they say.

It wasn't long until her mom moved to Seattle permanently. That left her dad alone in New York City, he would visit them in Seattle from time to time, but he was quite content to keep traveling the world. For some reason, Shelia couldn't connect with him although he tried to understand her love of practicing medicine. Wanting to help children was something that appealed to her while doing her residency.

One day she was assisting one of the doctors with helping an eight-year-old boy with some tummy issues. The first thing they did was to take all his vitals, then ask a series of questions. Shelia remembered being about eight years old and at the doctor's office. She wasn't feeling well; maybe she thought she was having severe headaches. Anyway, her mom went into the room with her as all parents do for young children under thirteen. The doctor would ask her mom all the questions while she just sat there on the table wondering. *Why isn't she asking me those questions?* When she noticed how her mentor treated the young boy with kindness, it inspired her to go in that field, the fact of treating children with respect or let's say as thoughtful humans was something she liked.

"Find a dad for those children" her mom would say.

Shelia wished that her mom would take a break from trying so hard to find her a man to marry. This wasn't on her radar right now, and she didn't perceive that it would ever change. Date night, was all she could think about. Not that she was excited, but that she was terrified to meet the man that her mom *hooked her up with.*

Here he comes she said to herself while looking out from her bedroom window upstairs. *He didn't look too bad* her mom said he worked for a Seattle radio station. It was something to do with keeping program sales objectives. Shelia wondered whether her mom even talked with this man or *PERHAPS FOUND HIM ON AN INTERNET SITE*! Either way, she had promised her that she would go out with him.

"Nice car," she said and then thought *now that was a smart thing to say, he'll probably think I'm so shallow to only like a guy for his car.* By opening her door, he was trying to show her what a gentleman he was. Indeed it was a very nice car, a BMW 520 sedan with all the bells and whistles. Off they went, he drove carefully, and seemed to be aware of not trying to speed or stop too quickly. These were things that some of his friends critiqued him on before this date. After all, he was excited about dating a doctor, plus she was quite beautiful too.

An evening of hanging out at a Seattle sports bar wasn't going to work for a doctor. So Charles found a very nice Italian restaurant on the north side of Bellevue. The funny thing is when you try to impress someone by not being yourself it could get messy. The night wasn't so bad. Charles tried to do all the right things and Shelia tried to be receptive, but her heart wasn't in it.

A smile from time to time seemed to encourage him. This was *walking* a *tight-rope* she thought, trying to seem interested but not give away the truth. I think tonight neither one was truly themselves. She did have a plan though, since he wasn't a disaster, at least not yet. Then she would go along with her mom's plans, except that there was no way she would marry him. *Hopefully* she thought that her mom would find something else to occupy her time with instead of playing matchmaker.

She gave him a little goodnight kiss, but not enough to encourage him too much, just enough to make him try harder. They dated for a few months, mostly only one night a week, and sometimes none. Somehow Shelia would always find a way to have something vital to do at work. It didn't take too long before Charles dropped his attempt to be something he was not.

On their fourth date which was about five weeks after the first one. He took her to one of his old hangouts in Seattle. It was a sports bar, and she had nothing against them. They were, however, a place where he felt he would feel comfortable and be himself. The guy wasn't an asshole, but when he got around his buddies, he did act like a child. She sat there watching him make a fool of himself. This wasn't the kind of man she wanted around her children.

Up to now she made it a point not to introduce him to her children. There was a required period she thought before that would happen and after tonight that wasn't going to happen! When returning home, she didn't speak, not even to answer his questions about if she was upset. When he pulled into the driveway, she told him that she would let herself in, and requested him to please never call her again.

Her mom was asleep and so were the children, so she didn't see any reason to wake them up. Plus she was so angry that it would be better to sleep it off. What a terrible night she had, her mind was racing with thoughts like; *men are all jerks, never again do I want to date,* and *I'm so mad at my mom for doing this to me.* Never was she raised to be negative but things like this soured her in life.

CHAPTER 8

A life lived in harmony is always the main purpose for us in our current existence on earth. This was now the time for George and Christa to begin their plan to create a wonderful life together. She liked the area, and with George spending time in the military he liked being home. He had a place in mind near a lake that he thought would make for a nice home to raise their family on. Three Rivers was a very peaceful and beautiful town to be linked to.

He couldn't have been lucky enough to find a hospital to practice in his hometown since he decided to pursue the orthopedic side of medicine. However, there was a town not too far away named Kalamazoo where he could find a position. Thankfully he did have another year left of residency and more classes to take to specialize in orthopedics.

For the next year, he and Christa worked together at the hospital, and life could not have been any better. George would go to school at night to work on his orthopedic credentials at Norte Dame. On the weekends they would travel to the lake area and look at the land around it. Hoping that one day they would purchase some land to build their home on. Children were in their plans, but they thought it would be better to wait for him to start practicing so that she could stay home to raise the children until they went to school.

These two were so close in all things, working, studying, and planning. Their thoughts were continually on trying to build their life together, but somewhat at the expense of the present moments together. George was starting to get burned out due to the late nights of work and then school. Christa was beginning to notice this, so that's when she told him they needed a break. Fortunately, it was summer, they went on a trip back up to Traverse City where he proposed to her, and relaxation was in order.

Their lives sort-of reset after spending another weekend up at Traverse City. They spent most of the time sleeping, relaxing, and of course, planning their future. Their plan was for George to finish his residency and orthopedic school. Both were going to work at the hospital until he finished school. Going to Pleasant Lake each Sunday became a regular thing for them. They loved getting away from work and school, plus being out in nature was so refreshing.

Bridges of Three Rivers

Spring was around the corner, and their wedding was quickly approaching. Christa's parents were more than happy to "foot the bill" because in their eyes George couldn't be more perfect. She was so close to George's mom that she invited her to go with her and her mom to pick out her dress. I don't believe George's mom Olivia has been that happy in a long time.

Her dress was perfect and it only took them three and a half hours to find it. Not white but it was light blue and she didn't want any other dress. This one was an original and was just so beautiful. It will be described later when they get married. Before taking Olivia home, Christa and her mom Peggy took her to their favorite tea shop for a late lunch.

Olivia was so happy for her son; she would spend most of his free time telling him about what a wonderful man his dad was. When she told him about his dad George Sr. she would always shed tears. George thought that this must be because she never remarried and moved on. Whether that was a mistake or not wasn't really for him to decide, but he wished she wouldn't cry every time. A week before his wedding he asked her not to tell any more stories about his dad because he didn't want to feel sad during a time that he was supposed to be happy. With a big smile and a hug she told him she understood and that was it.

There seemed to be so many things to do with so many arrangements. When Christa was with George, she tried her best not to be so stressed about them.

Sometimes he would laugh about it until she set him straight that it wasn't funny. Being the understanding, reevaluating man he was, he quickly shifted his attention to helping her calm down. George offered to help with the arrangements only to be told that she and her parents were taking care of them.

Spending time with his mom was such a help with Christa almost going out of her mind. George's mom helped him understand what she was going through and to understand that a wedding is one of the biggest events in a young woman's life. He understood and took all of his mom's advice to heart. Knowing that being there for her and lending an ear was all she needed because everything was going to be okay.

Spring in Michigan is very beautiful, not to mention that by an unexpected blessing Dr. Fritz knew someone that had a lovely home on one of the largest lakes in southern Michigan. This was made available to them a few months before. Christa went into high gear to make the arrangements. Then D-day arrived and she was ready, but so nervous, very nervous.

Birds were chirping, wind blowing lightly, everything green and beautiful. The music started, she looked down the path in front of him. His best man looked at him and gave him a thumbs-up. She was walking towards him holding onto her dad's arm and they both were walking slowly. A small tear of joy trickled down her cheek, but she's too far away for him to see it.

While walking by, all the ladies, and the men were looking at her. Her gown was exquisite, the light blue didn't alter how beautiful the sky was, but they seemed to blend so well. The cut was something that only the finest Taylor could do to make it work and look so good. From behind, the congregation let out a sigh, in unison for how wonderfully awesome the colours looked on her tail.

All was quiet, it seemed like the wind had stopped, the birds didn't even chirp, and George could only hear his heartbeat. They stopped right in front of him; the minister asked *who gives the bride away?* George looked on intently like he wasn't sure who would answer him and then Christa's dad said: *"I do."* Almost a laugh came out because George thought *aren't those our lines?* He smiled at her and said to himself *be serious these aren't... stop that!* George wasn't a cut-up, but he was so happy that day that he even acted funny.

Reality time, Christa stepped forward and stood on the other side of the minister. He started to read the vows, George looked right into her eyes, her eyes did all they could to welcome his imagination in. No rehearsed words, no change in the traditional vows. Both listened intently to his words and making sure their mouths were wet. They waited patiently to answer his fundamental question and with a resounding *I do!*

Finally, the crowning moment, placing the rings on their fingers, and then hearing *you may kiss the bride.*

Later in their reception which was full of friends and family dancing. The night was perfect, they were so beautiful, young and certainly meant for each other. Their parents were so happy that Olivia and Peggy even danced together. Everyone was having a great time, she threw the bouquet, and one of her best friends caught it. Dr. Fritz spent some time with them, exchanged hugs, kisses, best wishes, and when she found out they were sneaking out she helped them. They walked by their parents and said their goodbyes then Dr. Fritz looked at them, handed them an envelope before they went out through the back door.

They got into the car unnoticed, because it was dark with no moon or stars. George started drive, but didn't notice what was done to their tires. Pedal on the gas and the car was going nowhere, but he didn't become angry instead he started laughing. They opened the doors, both got out and looked at the car and noticed that there were half watermelons placed under the wheels. The outside lights came on, and people exited the building rushing to their car, all cheering and then several people lifted up the car and removed the watermelons.

On Pleasant Lake their home was being built and they couldn't imagine why things were going so well for them. That's not uncommon for people that are giving, caring, and grateful. They aren't aware of the laws of the universe, like the one that states *whatever you put out will come back to you in equal or greater amounts.* It doesn't matter either way these two liked being kind and friendly to everyone.

Home on the lake, George got a job in South Bend working with a practice that does knee, hip, and shoulder replacement. Christa worked at a hospital closer to their home but was looking for a nurse position at a pediatric clinic. That weekend they were moving into their home after all those years of waiting and planning.

George and Christa were so much in love that they did everything possible together and time spent on the lake was very therapeutic for them. They spent the warm months swimming, fishing, and boating. When Jack Frost blew in, they would enjoy ice skating. This home had that and much more going for it along with being right near the lake too.

One Saturday in late July they were sitting on the back porch sipping tea and watching the sun go down over the lake. Both relaxing thinking about their day and how grateful they were for all the blessings they had. They had just celebrated their fourth anniversary a couple of months ago. George had looked over his checklist that he had made many years before. He noticed that the one thing they were missing was children. Maybe Christa didn't think about that since she had been working at a pediatric clinic for over two years.

Thinking to himself *I wonder if I should bring up the subject of children and does she even want any?* These thoughts were racing in his head. So instead of just coming right out and saying it, he found a way to break the ice. "Darling, did you know that Bill and Allison were having their first child in the fall?"

"You mean Dr. Bill from your practice?"

"Yes him, they have only been married for two years now."

The porch was quiet, except for the crickets; I suppose the rain was coming soon. George thought *oh boy, now why did I say that?* Holding his hand, Christa looked him in the eye and said, "Do you want children, Mr. Esperanza?"

"Yes I do, and you look like the beautiful angel to give them to me."

She laughed and said, "you silly man, angels don't have children."

"Well, I guess you can be the first."

Within three months she was pregnant with their first child. He took very good care of her and his mom Olivia moved in with them. George's brother had finished college and then enlisted into the Air Force as a Lieutenant. The time came for Olivia to sell the house; she did not like being alone, now that her second son was gone.

When she was seven months pregnant, Christa went to town for her baby check-up. Olivia went with her and drove the car. The weather was cold, and there was a snow storm on the way. They had calculated that it shouldn't hit until later that evening so that they would be alright. The check-up confirmed the baby was fine, the mother was doing great, and the future grandma was happy.

Driving out of town took some time because of traffic. The girls thought they had better go a little faster than usual to make up for the lost time. The roads were fine, but up ahead there was some traffic on the two-lane road. Olivia slowed down when she spotted a semi-truck about half a mile ahead of her. Then from nowhere a pick-up truck just darted out from behind the truck. Olivia tried to slow down, but there were cars closely behind her. Without any time to assess the situation, she turned right because this pick-up was hell-bent on overtaking the semi-truck. And off they went into a ditch.

CHAPTER 9

With her mom there full-time, Shelia was contented. The children were looked after, and she could concentrate on her practice. Her mom backed-off from trying to find her a husband, so that debacle was over. And it's not that she didn't think about finding someone. In life people get lonely and being so young there was a lot of life ahead of her.

At work she took good care of her patients and this was one of the quintessential examples of throwing yourself into your work. Now that's not a bad thing we should give our total attention and energy to whatever we are doing at the moment. Work was fulfilling her need to occupy a good portion of her time. During the weekends her mom would always have some little adventure planned for them to do.

Steven was in school so only Julie stayed home with grandma. *He looked more and more like his daddy everyday* Shelia thought as she watched him put his shoes on. Shelia was so happy that even with her busy schedule she was still available to teach him how to tie the shoelaces. Grandma was doing a good job with Julie by teaching her to *go on the potty* just like mommy did for Steven two years before.

Life in Redmond was pretty nice, and she wasn't alone, her mom and the children were there. It had been two years, and Steven was seven, Julie five and in kindergarten. Her mom missed being with her daddy, and his health was starting to deteriorate. Being well educated, especially in the medical field, she realized that her daddy didn't have many years left. After talking with her mom, they both decided that, with the kids in school, maybe grandma should have granddad retire in their condo in Seattle with her.

Now life was changing for Shelia. She would get the kids up, dress them for school, and then drop them off. The only difference was that with her mom in Seattle she couldn't be there when school was over. Fortunately, Shelia was not on call very often so the kids could go right to her office after school, where she took them to a local after-school daycare for a couple of hours. This place was very good for them, it was fun, structured, and they could finish their homework with someone there to help them.

Some of Shelia's girlfriends at work, both nurses, weren't married but seemed to enjoy each other's company. They liked men but not romantically, so Shelia wondered if maybe she should try that lifestyle? That night she was going on a double date with them, and a friend they wanted to introduce her to. This friend was also a doctor, only that she was from Bellevue.

There was something different about this situation, she liked girls, but she was not sure about it. Her mindset was to go out with some friends and have fun. Her date that night seemed nice but about six years older than her, *so let's see what happen*s she thought. Not wanting to seem too obvious, they decided to go to a nice restaurant first, then some dancing later. The conversation was peppy enough, her friends acted like this was old hat, and Shelia still didn't find where this would work for her. Being girlfriends was great, but thinking of them romantically wasn't working.

Her number one goal was always to be the best friend she could be. These girls were so good to her and they knew that it was only experimental what Shelia was doing. With that said, they finished dinner, and went to the local Holiday Inn where they had dancing every weekend. Girls can always dance with each other and most people think it's cute. She was having fun dancing, especially since her date knew how, and both traded places to lead.

"Interesting" that was all she had to say to her friends Monday at work. A weekend spent together at the spa, dancing, dining, and some romance. Never thinking about another woman that way, she appreciated the familiarity of knowing what a woman wanted. She chuckled to herself and said *she wasn't a bad kisser. Let's see where this will go* she thought and continued to date her new friend Jenny.

Juggling her work and the children was never a problem until now. Dating Jenny was fun, she could make Shelia laugh, and with all that had happened to her in her life that was good. Some time went by, and with Shelia's schedule being busy, it was fortunate that the kids who seemed to like Jenny. Then once in a while Jenny would help with watching them. Shelia's dad was sick so she would go and see him whenever possible.

It wasn't that long before her mom called her with some bad news about the death of her dad and it happened so quick that she was very sad about losing him. Jenny volunteered to stay at her home and take care of the children. This was needed so much during this time because Shelia's mom needed her in her time of grief. This show of support helped Shelia to love Jenny even more. Shelia made for her mom all the burial arrangements. Since Shelia was not interested in running her daddy's business, they decided to sell it.

There were many companies eager to buy the business, so it didn't take long for the family's lawyer to draw up the papers. Most of the money went into a trust fund for the children which they would be given when they reached the age of maturity. The family decided that age to be twenty-five. Her mom's health wasn't that great, so they agreed to have her live in a costly nursing home in Bellevue. Shelia liked this because that way she wouldn't have to cross the bridge over Lake Washington, plus Jenny lived and worked in Bellevue.

Couples fight then they make-up or they break-up. These girls loved each other; they certainly helped each other, so why was their relationship not going anywhere? Well, this is the nineties, and the people of the gay community didn't have the right to marry. Their relationships were mostly kept a secret or very lose and free. Jenny had been in this environment for over ten years now, and she had her little shortcomings.

After all the family business was settled Shelia asked her mom what she thought about her relationship with Jenny. She seemed to be aware of it, and her thoughts were *if it makes her happy, and they love each other then why not.* That was the inspiration Shelia was looking for to ask Jenny to move in with her. Fortunately, Jenny was renting an apartment in the Bothell area, so she bought out her remaining two months of the lease, and moved right in.

They raised the children together and Jenny was the best companion she'd ever had. They were now two women doctors raising a little boy and a little girl. They did a lot of things together and the children were now seven and ten years old. Both children wanted to go to summer camp for four weeks. This was a perfect time for Jenny and Shelia to enjoy some time off together. All of them needed a vacation. The girls decided to spend their time doing things. There were spas, tennis, horseback riding, and even some skydiving. Shelia was really up for some adventure and Jenny was more than eager to do it with her.

They started their journey by driving around fifty-five miles an hour. It was in the country and the roads were narrow with deep ditches.

Two motorists stopped and quickly called 911, but couldn't get near the flipped car that was now on fire! Emergency vehicles arrived within three minutes and they quickly went into action putting the fire out. Both passengers were removed, put on gurneys, and loaded into the ambulance.

Both patients were rushed into the emergency room and straight into the burn unit. On these machines they were hooked up to make them somewhat stable. Doctors looked on while doing all they could to help them and found their selves disheartened about the injuries. Scrambling around, trying everything they could in the burn unit, but to no avail.

Why were they late? He thought, but didn't know where they were! Calling the doctor's office he was told they left over three hours ago. His mind was racing with this thought *what do I do, what do I?* Minutes that seemed like hours went by and all the fear he held inside finally subsided enough to allow this thought. *I need to call the police!* He hurriedly searched the phone book, running through the pages not knowing to look under city, county or just police. Then it came to him *dial 911 stupid.*

When the phone rang he tried to gain his composure, then the operator answered *911 what's your emergency?* After letting out a deep breath, he said "my wife and mother are missing."

The dispatch told him that she was transferring him over to the emergency police department. Not understanding what that meant, but right now he couldn't bother himself with that thought. A Sargent Webb answered on the other end and asked what his concern was. George went into details giving his wife and mother's full names.

Trying his patience, the officer didn't have any information then. However there were a few accidents and other emergencies that day, so without their names showing up, he wouldn't elaborate on them. Pacing the living room George had an even better idea. *Call the hospital and* that's just what he did. The desk nurse had just taken over her shift and was being briefed on all the patients. When Dr. Esperanza called she recognized his name because they had worked together before. He didn't want to ask for fear of the answer, but he did anyway "are my wife and mother there?"

She looked through the daily log and found their names. Noticing that they were in the intensive care unit and earlier they were in the burn unit. The phone then went silent while she did more research only to find that their conditions weren't stable. Remembering about how to break bad news to someone without causing them stress, she then told him that he needed to go and talk with their doctor.

Positive, be positive, he kept telling that to himself, waiting, praying, then making deals with God. All this was happening when he didn't even know anything just that they were there that night. Being a realist, he knew that something had to be wrong because being in the emergency room isn't a playground. He drove to the hospital carefully and that he was scared didn't help things.

He parked in one of the doctors' spaces and hurriedly rushed inside. He rushed to the nurses' desk looking for his friend, he spotted her! She saw him waving and she quickly walked over, and requested him to sit down for just a minute. She paged one of the doctors to come out and discuss with him the situation. A sudden calm came over him that he hadn't felt before. It wasn't pleasant, but then again it wasn't horrific either. Just as this feeling passed, he was greeted by one of the doctors. "Doctor Esperanza?"

"Yes, that's me. Do you have any word on my family? When can I see them?"

"Let's step into my office and I will explain."

This isn't good he thought. In his office, he explained to George all that had happened in the accident then described their condition when they arrived. George sat through all this and then a cold chill came over him. This doctor's final words to him were "I'm so sorry Doctor Esperanza..."

A couple of weeks went by, George and his brother buried their mom. At the same time, they buried Christa and their unborn child. When that was over he would get on with his life. Does anyone think it's that easy? I certainly don't think so. I'm not too sure he would ever be over this. His life was about to go into a tailspin especially since his brother was only there a few days before returning to duty.

He showed up for work only a few days after the funeral. His boss at work took him aside to explain that he would need to take some time off, and not return until he understood what had happened. Knowing that this wouldn't be easy, he told him to take as much time as he would need, and to feel free to contact him anytime. This could be good or it could very well be a bad thing.

His thoughts on his first day on extended leave were; *the ceremony was beautiful in the cathedral. The minister was gracious in his eulogy of my mom. I was impressed with how he told her story of raising two boys after her husband of only four years was killed in war.* His mind went blank for several seconds then he spoke aloud and said "mom I love and miss you and I know you are with my wife and our baby in heaven." That was as far as he wanted to stretch his thoughts and in no way did he want to recall Christa's name or their baby's.

He just sat around at home being sad and doing nothing. This is what he thought his life would now be defined as. *Sure mom had her moments and raising us on the farm kept her busy. But she was so young and beautiful. I never understood why she didn't find someone else and remary.* After thinking about that he paused and drew a blank to that question.

He had a late night drinking scotch on the rocks. He wasn't an alcoholic but did like an occasional drink. With Christa he preferred wine, but now he didn't want her memory to be stirred. Remembering Job from the Bible, he didn't want to be angry with God, so he thought *why God, why did you do this to me?* After more drinking, a fear that he would curse God weighed heavy on him that night.

Days of depression engulfed him. Some ladies from church brought him food. Since he was unshaven and barely clean, these ladies were a little bit afraid to approach him. He spent most of the day by the lake fishing and drinking beer. Never did he imagine that this could ever happen to him, he said to himself *I didn't have this in my plans.*

He walked around the big lake to calm down, tears flowing like a South Carolina storm. Choking on his tears and sobbing, made it difficult to see where he was going. Broken hearted he yelled out in the night "my life was all set, what will I do now?"

Bridges of Three Rivers

Waiting for God to answer is like waiting for the wind to blow, it will blow when it damn well pleases! Soon enough his answer came in the form of a tree! He was turning the corner around a couple of boats on the shore. Crying again, hurting as bad as he had since the tragedy, then he fell to his knees. When he noticed this tree it wasn't just any tree, but it wasn't the tree that he had noticed. What he had noticed was that as the wind blew through the leaves this tree would bend and then return upright, he realized how precious life was, and as sad as he was he was still alive!

He never had a good night sleep for several days until that night. His sleep was so good that he awoke the next morning not only completely happy but also completely conscious. With his feet on the floor, he said "I'm going to be grateful, no matter what happens, and I will believe that there is a better life out there for me." He drank some sports drink, went for a jog around the lake and noticed the tree again. He went back home showered then made breakfast, sat down, and made a plan to travel.

After conversing with his brother, he agreed to his plan. George made arrangements for his brother to step in and check on things while he was away. Not that his brother wasn't away, but he seemed receptive to vacationing there, especially since he liked the fishing on the lake. The first thing was to go back to the office for a couple of weeks to work out an extended leave notice.

When he went back to work, George performed all his duties just like before, with good manners and doing the best for his patients. As the week progressed, he noticed how much he needed to get away from all the familiar faces and places. Christa's memory would take time to heal, he loved her so dearly that he thought he shouldn't give himself to someone so deeply again? That thought bothered him, and he prayed that it would lead to something better.

After preparing for the day of his departure he spent some time visiting Dr. Fritz. She was a dear friend ever since she chose him for his residency. He invited her over to the lake where they spent hours sitting and talking. She reflected a lot of light back to George about all he had been through and how all of life is a test. She agreed with him on the plan he set out to do, knowing that this would open up his eyes and his heart even more. They said their goodbyes and he left the next day for his journey.

CHAPTER 10

Jenny wanted a commitment from her, but Shelia wasn't sure if this was what she wanted. Sure it is fun and wonderful to have a companion like Jenny, but there were a lot of difficulties to work around. That night Jenny wanted to argue with her and the reason wasn't quite clear. Shelia tried to talk to her and explain why she didn't feel the same way. For the sake of their relationship and the help they gave each other Shelia wanted Jenny to stay.

"So, you want us to be together as friends, but you also want to have the option of dating someone else?" Jenny asked while waving her hands.

"No not exactly." I don't have anyone in mind. I was just concerned about what if we met someone else."

That statement didn't sit well with Jenny, she had moved in, helped out during difficult times and now this! I don't know what Shelia was thinking, other than her looking at her children grow older, which made her think about what might have been if Brad wasn't such an idiot. *That was water under the bridge* she said to herself.

She wanted to forget about the argument she had with Jenny. Thus, Shelia was ready to take the kids over to Bellevue to visit their grandmother. While driving there Steven asked her questions about their daddy and why they weren't together. She had never worked these questions out as to what she would say to them when that day came. Now this was that day, so *what can I tell him about his daddy, he was so young when we divorced?*

Looking over at him in the passenger seat she said: "dear, your daddy and I loved each other, but we found that there were a few things we lacked in our relationship."

"What were they, mommy?"

She went on to delicately tell him things like they couldn't agree on certain topics. Luckily Steven didn't press too much, but he wanted to know more about his daddy. Therefore, she said he was a successful businessman, handsome, could shoot a basketball pretty good, and that he liked flying. All was well until he asked her "why don't we see him? Is he dead like grandpa?"

Oh boy, this drive is turning into a disaster. She said "alright then, he's not dead like grandpa, he's just really busy working and he lives far away."

Hoping that it would suffice him, instead she could see that it was getting him a little bit confused. That's when she told him that adults do a lot of things that don't make sense. It seemed to bring some calm to him when she told him that she was sure he would visit them one day.

The day was nice, not too nice, but for Seattle, it was one of the best days in over a week. Her mom was so happy to see her and the kids. The thoughts of her husband of over thirty years being gone caused her to be depressed. Shelia talked with her about her problems with Jenny who wanted more of a commitment from her. Her mom didn't seem to understand their relationship very well. In her mind, if two people wanted to commit to each other, then they would just get married.

The kids were so occupied watching TV, which gave Shelia the time to talk with her mom about a lot of things. One of the subjects was what to do with the money from dad's business? Other than the monies set aside for the kids, when they reached twenty-five, there will still be a good portion left over. Although her residence was very nice, *it should be for what I'm paying* thought Shelia. Nevertheless, her mom was starting to feel lonely; this was something she made known through her talk about her dad, and not having any family around.

Bridges of Three Rivers

Julie got up to go to the restroom and on her way back grandma wanted to see her. After Julie walked over to her to hug her, she then moved back to kiss her, and noticed that she was crying. For a twelve-year-old to see her grandma cry wasn't a good thing. Soon she was crying too, this disturbed Shelia, and Steven so much. Both were trying to inquire what was wrong, and the funny thing was that Julie said: "I don't know."

It was time for the family to have their intervention! Shelia started by asking her mom why she was crying. Her Mom told her that she just felt it was too soon for her to be alone without family with her dad gone. Shelia then decided that she would make the necessary arrangements to have her move back in with them. Feeling that she was doing the right thing, Shelia thought *maybe this will give Jenny an opportunity to find someone that is more ready for a commitment?*

However, Shelia kept her thoughts to herself, while on the drive back home. The children were very excited about grandma moving back in with them. Markedly, she didn't mention what Jenny would think about that. Even though Jenny and her mom got along very well, Shelia believed it could be a problem for her not knowing what she was doing, but Shelia was in a way putting the idea to Jenny of her moving out.

Back home she started making the arrangements to move her mom back in that day. Somehow she forgot to mention this to Jenny, so when she somehow found out, there was a problem. When she came home late that night, dinner was missing, and Jenny just mopped around the house. The kids were upstairs getting ready for bed when Jenny asked her "when is your mom moving back in?"

"Oh my god, I am so sorry I didn't mention it to you."

"That's okay, I'm not against it. I'm just hurt you didn't tell me."

This was a tedious situation between them. Probably it was a continuation of their conversation a week earlier about commitment. *Somehow things will work out;* she thought and wasn't too concerned about it. Truth be told she loved Jenny, but the possibility of committing to their relationship just wasn't there. Her mom would be moving back in less than a week.

Jenny and the kids went to get Shelia's mom on Saturday and came back with her. This might have been her way of showing support for Shelia's decision. Jenny loved the kids, and all they could talk about was their grandma moving back in, so she thought *if you can't fight them, then join them.* They walked in with only one mission, to get their grandma, and bring to her home. On opening the door, Shelia's mom noticed Jenny and made a point to say hello to her. Oh hell, she told her to come over, and hug her. This really made Jenny feel good, so she smiled, and walked over to get her hug.

All of them were getting along well and her mom's role didn't change from before. She started getting the kids up, ready for school, and even packing their lunch. Having something to do and being responsible for that was like medicine to her soul. Not that Jenny and Shelia weren't doing a great job, they were.

Now they found themselves with extra time on their hands. Jenny wasn't ready to be idle, so she started asking Shelia to go out dancing more. At first, Shelia liked the idea, but there was a drawback to this, and that was too much time together! Yep, too much of a good thing gets you thinking, and both girls were analyzing their relationship.

At work they both had different thoughts, Shelia's were, *I love Jenny, but I believe if I'm going to commit to someone I think I want it to be a man. Something that I'm missing, maybe it's the yin and yang thing?* While Jenny's thoughts were, *what does she mean she wants to see other people? We have fun together; we go dancing, take care of the kids, and even share medical interests.*

It seemed like a boomerang to her. This wasn't anything she had dealt with before and how she would do it was news to her. It all happened when the phone rang on a Saturday. Jenny answered and on the other end was Shelia's ex-husband Jake. Yes Jake, the man that was let off the hook when it came to child support, and at the time he didn't care about visitations. So why is he calling now after several years of being out of their lives? Well, it's all about the money. He found out that her dad died. Mind you it did take a little while before he did.

Armed with this knowledge he immediately tried to use the children to his advantage. He didn't know however that Shelia had a female partner or that her mom was there too. He didn't say much to Jenny, so she dispatched the phone to Shelia like it was a hot potato. When he started asking her about her dad she knew what was up. She quickly told him that he had no inheritance from her family. This was a fact that he didn't even try to deny, but what he tried to do was to use gaining visitations of the children as a way of extorting money from her.

The United States does not pay extortion money and neither does Shelia. Telling him no wasn't enough and he kept bugging her, harassing her, and threatening to ask for child visitations if she didn't give in to his demands. He was getting desperate, but that didn't matter. Even though his calls and threats were causing a strain on Shelia's life, the children didn't know their dad was in town, and this secret was something that she didn't know if it could be kept for long.

At work she would receive phone calls from him, begging and pleading for money. This was so bad that she contemplated giving him money, but she knew it wouldn't stop there. This was one bad situation she would have to ride out. On a walk break, she had a thought. *Maybe if I moved where he couldn't find me then I wouldn't be bothered by him?* When she approached her mother with the idea, she said it was not a bad idea, so the three talked about it. It was Shelia's idea, so she was for it, Jenny not so much, she didn't want to leave her home, and her mom didn't care as long as she was with her girl and grandchildren.

Weeks went by, and still, there were no signs of Jake letting up. He lived just north of Seattle, probably about one hundred and twenty miles away. Three times visitations a week or so were well worth it to get some of her daddy's money. The children were starting to hear little bits of something happening, but they didn't know what it was just yet. So the day came when she asked Jenny and her mom if they had any ideas of where to move.

Jenny quickly said "now if you move more than seventy-five miles from Seattle then I don't believe I'll be going."

Her mom then spoke and said "dear Jenny, Shelia needs to get as far away from this loser as she can, so don't try and stop her."

Jenny felt like she had just been spanked and not in a good way. Nevertheless this would be a pivotal moment for all of them. Shelia didn't want anyone's feelings to be hurt, so she asked: "mom do you have any ideas?"

"Yes I do, we have relatives in Michigan. We could move there, that's well over two thousand miles away."

Jenny said "well you can count me out of that move."

"I know Jenny and I'm sorry, but I think it would be better to move away from here to get away from Jake." Shelia then looked at her and said "you have been such a good friend and partner all these years. It will pain me to lose your companionship, so I ask you to move with us. I will take care of the finances and you can take your time finding another practice."

Two weeks later Jenny moved back to Bellevue and severed her ties with Shelia. This was a blow for her and the kids because they loved Jenny very much. Grandma spent most of the day with Julia wiping her tears trying to soothe her heartache. Where they were going was very new to them, even her mom had not been there in over forty years.

They made sure the movers had everything packed before they set out on their seven-day journey. Sure, it could be made in three days, but Shelia wanted to enjoy the trip and make some stopovers along the way. She upgraded to a Cadillac Escalade for the long journey, with only their suitcases in the back. Shelia was doing all the driving, and it would be about three hundred miles a day.

Bridges of Three Rivers

First stop, Boise, Idaho and after spending the night in Boise, the next day they stopped in the Salt Lake City, Utah area. Where they did some site seeing, spent another night and drove to Denver, Colorado. They saw the Rocky Mountains and a few other sites. They spent the night in Denver then drove to Kansas City, Missouri and spent the night there. They ate some great KC barbecue and the next morning they took off for St. Louis, Missouri. The next morning in St. Louis they went up into the arch and enjoyed the view from six hundred and thirty feet! They had one more stop and that would be Indianapolis, Indiana. They spent the night there and the next day toured the Indy 500 racetrack. After the racetrack, they drove up to a small town called Coldwater, Michigan.

Coldwater was the area where Shelia and her mom had relatives. They rested that night because the following day they would meet their relatives. After waking up they drove into town where there was a very old restaurant that served a good American breakfast. Shelia's extended family loved the place and suggested that they meet there. The kids found some distant cousins to hang around with, her mom reconnected with some old cousins, and Shelia seemed to fit right in with her family from far away.

CHAPTER 11

He promised his practice that he would return in two years after going on this adventure. That day he would be a doctor working with the Doctors without Borders organization. It was similar to the military in that he spent a few days getting processed. The first day consisted of more paperwork, mostly promising not to sue if he were to become injured. The better part of the next day was a medical exam to include a series of shots. Then the last day he was to be issued his gear for traveling, which consisted of a sleeping bag, a cot, a backpack, sidearm, and some desert clothing.

George finished with all the in-processing and then went on to board the plane. On the long flight from Chicago to London, England he slept and thought about what he had lost. *Christa, I miss you and wish you could be here with me, or instead, I wish we were both back in our home on the lake. Our life seemed so perfect, I just don't understand the master plan, and this world is filled with such tragedies. I suppose if we didn't have bad things in this world then we wouldn't appreciate the good things that we have. Sometimes I wonder if I could have instead taken your place if that would have sufficed.*

Soon he was at Heathrow Airport, taking some time to relax while waiting three hours for his next flight. Sitting at a coffee bar and sipping some espresso, he couldn't help but notice a young couple sitting at a table. She must have been six months pregnant. All he could do was think about Christa and how happy he was when she was pregnant knowing that his first child was on the way. But all that had been taken from him along with his mother. Maybe, just maybe, George would find some peace in the joy of helping others.

He had a happier time in his life, that was for sure. He found himself in this camp deep in the jungles of Africa. While accessing the place, the first thing that came to his mind was some of the places his fellow PJ's went to rescue downed pilots. The one mission he was on had similarities to this place. Other than the one mission, George spent a lot of time training, and that training was as real as it could be. With this in mind, he was quite confident that his military training would help him in this endeavor.

Find a tent to drop off my duffle bag, then locate the hospital, those were his thoughts after arriving at camp Peacock. Even though it seemed like the military visually, it certainly wasn't organizationally. He found this out very quickly when he asked who he was to report to. One of the doctors laughed and asked "why do you need to report to anyone?"

"No, who do I see about my duties here?"

Again the doctor said "well, we all do what we can around here, and some of us are a jack of all trades."

George was then able to fully understand that this outfit was not run like the military. However, some schedules were to be kept mainly to cover the hospital through the sleeping hours. He went back to his tent and met another member there that bunked close by. His name was Calvin, who was not a doctor, but an engineer from the army, and the civilian world.

His first week at camp Peacock became a little bit trying. I guess what he was doing to bring about a calmness seemed to backfire often. On the third day, he questioned himself; *what am I doing here? Does this all make sense to leave a comfortable home and job for?* He tried his level best not to get caught up in the negativity. By the end of the week he had realized that the job was to do your best with what you had. What a lesson to learn in life for George at the time. It was almost seven days before his thoughts were quiet enough to remember what brought him here in the first place.

Poverty was deep in this place, only a handful had any wealth and there were the warlords who kill, and steal all the wealth. George and his compadres would spend many nights asking these questions only to find no apparent answers. Most nights he would just lay there and think *why doesn't the international community step in? The least they can do is bring in a police force to stop these warlords.* Many good people had the same thoughts and didn't understand that it's all a game. A game in which we all learn our parts, perform our roles the best we can, and then hopefully when the final curtain falls we get a standing ovation.

That day, the group of twelve went out to provide food, clothing, and medicine to the locals. Being doctors they weren't meant to defend themselves, but they usually carried a sidearm. Their group consisted of three doctors, four nurses, and five members to provide security. This group of five that provided security were usually two engineers and three others that were trained in weapons and security or both.

George was well equipped to perform this work. After a couple of months he found his groove. That day, he helped a little girl who had an infected left leg that was getting so bad it would need to be amputated! His expertise in combat surgery and his orthopedic knowledge helped him when he cleaned the bone out to remove the infection. He then put some chemical compound that would ensure that the infection didn't come back. In doing this, her pain was reduced to an amount that was handled with a simple aspirin. Before she left with her leg repaired and in a cast, she gave George a big hug, and then told him she loved him in her language.

The night was approaching, so they needed to wrap things up. When the sun went down the village people retreated to their shacks and prayed that the warlords wouldn't visit them. Also, the volunteer workers needed to get back to the safety of their camp. Loading up and finishing their work, all were heading out as the sun started its quick move down the horizon. Yes, I know the sun doesn't move it's the earth that rotates, but it sounds more romantic to say the sun drops down.

On the road, the warlords were racing behind them, still out of gun range, but closing in rapidly. They had a lot of this timed out, as to how fast they could go, and how fast the warlords traveled. Also, they factored in the distance of their weapons, and to that of the warlords. A few minutes later, the bullets started flying towards them as they were racing to their camp. Some of the security detail started firing back, but only carefully placed shots, they didn't want to waste too many rounds. Ping ping was the sound of bullets reaching the truck at the end of the line. The camp had its gates opened and they were then firing off several mortar rounds to slow down the warlords.

Thankfully there was still some distance between them and the warlords. Vroom! And into the gate, they flew in almost like a naval fighter landing on a carrier!

He made some new friends that would last for a lifetime. George thought about all he had lost that night back home. Caught up in helping these people he found a sense of purpose beyond the day to day survival. *There is a higher purpose in this life when you can help another it seems to give you back more than what you give out.* Knowing that what he was feeling was a big part of healing and then finding a greater goal made it much easier to do.

After working for over fourteen months, George knew that he was over the halfway mark. He and Calvin became good buddies and that day they had a new arrival in the tent. A doctor from Chicago joined them, and his name was John. John quickly befriended both of them. The three were almost inseparable for the next ten months. Having limited supplies, volunteering to be there, and then finding great satisfaction in what they were doing.

All this reminded John of something he wanted to do one day. John grew up watching MASH on TV and he wanted to be like Hawkeye Pierce. Both George and Calvin also watched the show as they grew up religiously. The three would sit in their bedding area drinking gin, and then reminisce about the show's funny scenes. It was these moments that meant so much to George and grounded his belief in the goodness of people.

George and John were like brothers working together. Sometimes they would talk with Calvin about possible improvements to some of their medical equipment. Calvin had a secondary engineering degree in medical devices. Calvin enjoyed receiving this information firsthand from the doctors, who performed these miracles with those tools. During this time Calvin kept an engineering book to document their input and any parts they experimented with.

The supplies were getting low, and the doctors relied heavily on the engineers to find substitutes. It hurt them so much to have to perform medical treatment without the needed medicines and equipment. George wrote home to his doctor friends and received some supplies, but they barely made a difference because the need was so great. Part of the job was to solicit funds and or supplies wherever possible.

This was when he learned that his mentor Dr. Fritz was a member of the Eastern Star. When she asked her fellow Stars to help, they went into action, and had the camp supplied with more than they needed. This didn't take long either and they spared no expense to do it. Not only was George happy to communicate with Dr. Fritz, I mean after all she approved of his venture, but he was also impressed with the Stars Masonic brothers too. Her lodge which was made up of both Eastern Stars and Masons did some glorious work for camp Peacock.

Bridges of Three Rivers

With only a few months left, George contemplated staying for another year. But not until he received word from his brother that he was not going to reenlist in the Air Force and that he would be coming home. That was half of the news that his brother sent. The other part was that he would be getting married in the spring. Putting two and two together, he realized how much he wanted to be there when his brother came home, and that if he stayed for another year, he would miss his brother's wedding. This wasn't going to happen, their parents were gone, and now they were the only family left. George was also going to be the best man.

So he finished his last three months with some exciting events. Like the time all the power went out, and they had to unbox the emergency generators. No one knew how to use these old relics accept a couple of the engineers remembered using some that were similar some twenty years before in the army. What a disaster, but when they all pulled together, it was marvelous to behold. Some new people came in during his two years, and a couple left. All were his friends, so each was treated as a brother or sister.

The whole plan was quite remarkable; they would help the local people with schools, hospitals, farming, and even their protection. With so much poverty it was a constant struggle to survive. George learned how to make the best of whatever the situation was at the time. He knew that wherever he went, he could always reflect on his time spent here for strength.

One of the nurses gained some of his attention, he even thought of maybe trying to love again, but the circumstances seemed to be so intense that he wasn't sure if this love was for real. He told this sweet nurse who caught his eye that it just couldn't work then, but maybe he would return in a year, and they could have another chance. She was from Argentina, so the logistics were awful anyway.

He had one last night with his buddies Calvin and John. They drank a lot of gin that night, mostly sad that he was leaving, but happy that he was going home to see his brother.

He took the truck and headed for the airstrip, then off to several connections before arriving at Heathrow airport in London. With the short flights and constantly moving around with his duffle bag, George didn't have time to think until he arrived at Heathrow. While on the flight across the big pond, otherwise known as the Atlantic Ocean, his thoughts were; *going back home after two years in Africa. I hope I can operate in a structured environment.* He took a few hours to nap until he heard the stewards calling for drinks.

After taking refreshments, his mind then wondered about the past; *I had everything I wanted, a beautiful wife, a baby on the way, our dream home by the lake, and my mom living with us. Then in one evening, it was all taken away from me. Now I feel stronger seeing how all people struggle with problems, knowing that we are not given more than we can handle.* Looking around him at all the different people on the plane he concluded his thoughts with; *I will continue to strive to be a better person and help my fellow human beings. Any way I can!*

CHAPTER 12

They rented a home in Coldwater before moving out there. Shelia flew with her mom and the kids, weeks before to look at some houses they had first selected from a realtor on the internet. Relocating seemed like the thing to do to help her find a new life, especially after the debacle with Jake. Jenny was a blessing and Shelia was so happy to hear that she met someone else. Someone they both knew, so that was a nice connection for them.

At first Shelia thought with the money they had she would want to stay at home with her mom. That didn't last very long, not that being at home with her mom wasn't great, because it was. However, her credentials as a medical doctor would go to waste if she decided to stay at home. She talked with her mom about the kids then other things and later spent some quiet time alone. There her thoughts were *I'm happy here, this is a nice town with relatives around, a beautiful home, the kids like the school, and mom seems to be happier with the small town atmosphere. So why am I not happy or at least contented? God if you're out there give me a sign, some direction to go on.* She went to the local cathedral with her mom and talked with the priest.

While in town one day she met a man who was a doctor at a local practice. He was married, but when she heard someone at this local coffee shop refer to him as doctor, she then told her mom that they needed to sit with him. Her mom obliged, he was sitting alone then Shelia introduced herself and her mom to him. She went on to tell him her story about going to school at Notre Dame, then doing her residency in the Seattle area. He told her about where he went to college and was working at a practice there in Coldwater. Then he went on to tell her about his wife and their three children. When she told him of her two children, they enjoyed telling tales of their children's exploits.

He had to go back to the office and said goodbye, but not before exchanging their contact information. During their conversation, this doctor informed Shelia of where she could go to look for a practice to join. This made her think and then while laughing her mom said: "dear I think you need to go back into medicine, being a stay at home mother isn't your calling."

Shelia was so pleased with her mom's honesty that she said while laughing with her "thank you so much for saying that, you know the truth shall always set us free." The following day Shelia set out to find a practice to join.

Shelia was back in the medical community working again. She hadn't realized how happy this made her. Taking it slow, she attended a party or two but still no dating, although she told herself that soon she would be ready. Reflecting on her relationships with Jake, and then Jenny, she didn't want to throw the baby out with the bath water. Because Jake was a jerk and Jenny was very sweet. Being a lesbian had its advantages and having had two children with Jake was certainly an advantage as a heterosexual.

She was working at a family clinic just outside of Elkhart, Indiana which wasn't a bad drive. It was about sixty miles with no traffic and some beautiful countryside to see. Life was starting to look up for Shelia except that she needed someone to share it with. On her drive to work one day she had a conversation with herself *okay are there any dating prospects at work?* Watching the horses in the field and the pretty red barns her answer came back to her *no, not really, maybe the nurse or receptionist. Wow, all the doctors are men, and both are married!*

Not letting the small pool of men nor the nondesire to travel down the lesbian path again discourage her. During the next few months she found plenty to keep her busy with the kids and school. She lay in bed at night looking out the window at the stars and the moon. Filled with hope, her thoughts before turning in were *I know he's out there so let us meet. I'm ready to love again.* Hugging her pillow as if it were her new man, her eyes would become heavy, and then close.

Peter's brother George was now home at the airport waiting for him, to drive to South Bend, and pick him up. He hadn't seen his brother in two years and there was so much he wanted to tell him. Also, he was excited to hear about his adventures in Africa. The distance from the lake was maybe an hour's drive plus or minus ten minutes. He pulled into the loading area at the airport, when he saw George walking up his thoughts were about how much he missed their mom, and the tragedy that took her and George's wife. That night there would be no talk of things that could bring sadness for he was too excited to see him again.

"George my brother, I'm so glad to have you back in the country."

"Thanks, little brother, I missed you a lot."

With only a duffle bag, George didn't take too long to load it, and to leave. On the drive home they were so excited to get up to speed talking with each other about what they've been doing the last two years. George was especially interested in this woman that his brother was going to marry in the spring. Both were talking so much neither had a thought to themselves.

Bridges of Three Rivers

With a long layover George was very tired, so as soon as they arrived at the house, he hugged his brother, and said "goodnight."

Both had the weekend off, so they spent each day out fishing on the lake. George told him about Africa, the people, the warlords, and the satisfaction of helping others. Peter described to him the girl he had met and was going to marry. Peter told him about meeting her in the city close to the base where he was stationed. Her daddy was a retired First Sargent from the 82nd Airborne in Fort Bragg, N.C. While Peter was stationed at Pope Air Force Base right next door. They meet at the community college that he was attending. At the college he was studying to get his contractor's license. The plan was for her to stay at her parents' house until the wedding which would be at her church.

All this good news helped George get motivated and excited about returning to his practice again. While driving in the morning, he decided to perform around five minutes of Om exercises. He was feeling very stimulated from head to toe, and his thoughts were, *all the equipment we didn't have over in Africa I will have here. It is going to be exciting to go back and see my friends at work. Today I want to think about them as my extended family.* He pulled into his parking space, got out of the car, put his hand in his pocket, grabbed his three gratitude stones, and said "I am so grateful for this day."

Bridges of Three Rivers

Imagine what it would have been like to go from having all these luxuries to not having any of them for two years? On returning home, you find yourself back with those luxuries again. You would certainly have a greater appreciation of them. It would take some time to get used to relating to his colleagues, but he would manage. With that said, there were a couple of new people brought in while he was gone. Among them were two new doctors; one man and a woman, three nurses; two women and one man, almost like a quota, but he was happy to see new faces.

It was fun meeting with the new doctors, one was doing her residency from Michigan, the other finished his in Chicago, and he was only going to stay a while until something opened up in the Chicago area. All three nurses were full time and from the area, like Notre Dame, Michigan State, and Purdue. That day his colleagues took him out to lunch, they left the new people back to watch over the shop, or so they told them.

Ah, his favorite place to have lunch was where they went. He didn't think to bring up the tragedy of what had happened over two years ago because he was too busy answering questions about Africa. Telling his stories of barely escaping the warlords several times and then when all their lights went out. For some reason, George became very good at telling these stories and it raised his spirits to see their faces light up when he told them about the chase scenes!

When their meal was almost over, he started telling them about the exploits of Calvin, and John. This got the group laughing when he would tell them about the tricks they would do and how they made their gin just like in the MASH series.

Being back home was never so special, and on his first drive there, he made his peace with Christa. *I do miss you and wish with all my heart that you could be here. Knowing that you are in a better place helps me, sometimes I wonder what our child looks like up there with you, and my parents.* He usually remained quiet as a way of waiting for an answer, not that one would come audibly, but maybe in the sign of a cardinal flying by or a willow tree waving. To him, it could be anything, but he just knew that she was there listening to him. *I'm going to say goodbye my dear and I have another favor to ask. If you feel it's the right time for me to find someone else, please give me a sign that could only come from you.*

Not everyone was excited about the new town. Julie had some problems with a particular little girl in school. Steven was fine, he was very outgoing, and didn't let other people bother him. Shelia asked her mom for advice on how to help Julie with her school problem. Her mom was very helpful and decided to be there when Shelia talked to her. It took a few weeks to take up the challenge finally, but once Julie started returning her insults with kindness and the little girl stopped. The two became best friends after three weeks.

Shelia was trying to meet the perfect man and that wasn't easy for her. She went out on a couple of blind dates, knowing that this was something she had said she would never do again, but she said *these are desperate times.* At least going out and mingling with other people was a perfect place to start.

She enjoyed working but the only limitation was the drive, she didn't like being over an hour away from home. As she was waiting to meet the right person, she didn't want to be too tied down in case she needed to move or commute, but those things will take care of themselves.

That day she would have enough issues to deal with, both good and bad. The school was about to be closed for the summer and she wanted to travel somewhere exotic with the family. Sitting on the back porch with her mom they started brainstorming on where to go that summer for a vacation. The Pacific Northwest was out of the question, *maybe France* Shelia thought. She suggested that idea to her mom, and it seemed to be a good one because she remembered going there several times with her dad, and even taking Shelia along once or twice. Also, they brought the children in to talk about their plans.

All were in agreement with France. Her mom wanted to freshen up on her French, so she did a three-week course online. After she had completed the course, she could speak French again, something she had learned a long time ago. With her knowledge back, she put together a plan to teach the others before their trip. Young children are so easy to teach, and their ability to retain information is mind-boggling.

For the next month, all the kids could talk about was going to France, seeing the Eiffel Tower, the Louvre Museum, and eating the great French cuisine that their, mom and grandma talked about. They would be closing school soon and then they had to wait a week before traveling. Shelia was encouraged by her mom to make sure everyone had updated passports some years earlier.

They were ready to take a chartered jet flying from Battle Creek, MI, to fly to Chicago to board on the plane. The tickets were for business class and a direct flight to Paris, France. The children had never flown overseas before, so this was an adventure especially looking out over the ocean.

The plane touched down at a very high speed, and then the engines roared in reverse, the captain turned sharp, and rolled to the ramp. Once their bags were gathered they all debarked from the plane and met in the lobby. They went downstairs to wait for their luggage. Julie was excited and said "Nous somme ici" which is French for "we are here."

Steven answered, "n'est-ce pas génial" which means "isn't it great?"

Bridges of Three Rivers

Their mom and grandma were very pleased with their use of the language.

Their driver was waiting downstairs very close to the luggage carousel. It didn't take too long because they were on a flight that didn't have many people on it. In the car and down the streets of Paris, they looked around and in the distance, they could see the Eiffel Tower. Even from a distance, it looked huge. The flight wasn't too uncomfortable, but the jet lag made them tired. They thanked the hotel when room service brought them a late dinner and they were all sleepy after eating.

The first day in Paris, they were up early and excited. Shelia was so happy to get away and enjoy life without any pressures. Lately, she had been working hard and trying to meet the next love of her life. On the drive to the Eiffel Tower, she sat in the back seat listening to Steven, and Julie talk about where they were going. While sitting, she thought; *maybe I should live off of daddy's money? After all, it had been wisely invested, and it will provide for our needs for many years to come.*

Steven said "Nous voilà!" here we are!

Julie forgot to use French and said "wow."

Speaking in French, her mom told her "it is okay, we just want to have fun using their common language." Their grandma confirmed that and also speaking in French told her to enjoy the tower. They went up to the top, looked around, felt a little dizzy, found the restaurant, and then ate lunch. What a view! They all admired the architecture and took lots of pictures. Julie couldn't wait to share them with her new friend who used to pick on her. They also visited the Louvre Museum and several other stops during the week. After visiting several places, they then boarded the plane back home.

They were back to southern Michigan, what a beautiful place France is lovely, and Paris is exquisite, but there is no place like home. And now Southern Michigan was their home. Shelia's family were enjoying themselves, spending at least the next two weeks talking about the vacation, especially away from Jake, and his constant interruptions.

At work there were some parties and there was also training happening. The following week Shelia was scheduled to go to a medical conference in Chicago. There she would be trained about some new ways of making sure to follow specific government guidelines that the FDA would approve. She would need to spend a few days there and her mom would take care of the children. It was good timing because the kids were at home during the rest of the summer. She was looking forward to mingling with the medical people there who hailed from the Midwest region.

CHAPTER 13

It was George, along with two doctors, and two nurses ready for the drive to Chicago in their rental. They booked five single rooms at the Marriott in Schaumburg, IL.

The drive to Chicago wouldn't take more than a couple of hours to get there. The doctors were men and both nurses were women. These women were married so George had no one to meet there. They were good company and they all had a good time talking while traveling. The traffic wasn't bad because they chose to leave on Sunday, that way they could be at the conference by 8 am without having to get up at four in the morning, and then deal with the traffic.

Schaumburg is a suburb of Chicago and its where the conference was being held. Nothing exciting to talk about, just a lot of tedious government regulations and stuff. However, all of them got a chance to meet other medical professionals from the northern

Indiana, southern Michigan area. This was for five days, so they would mingle around during lunch and meet other people.

George met some dentist from nearby Jackson, MI. These guys were a riot, they talked a lot about hunting, and how some people needed to be careful out in the woods during deer season. That evening he met a nurse named Susan from the Elkhart, IN area, she worked for a family practice. She was alone, so when he asked her if she was alone she replied that she was with a group, but she accepted his invitation to sit with him. They sat and talked for a while, then went to their rooms for the night.

The next day George was having lunch with a colleague when Susan spotted him. She waved at him and he then invited her and her friend to come sit down with him. George introduced his fellow doctor named John to them and Susan introduced her doctor friend whose name was Shelia. George enjoyed talking to Susan, and she was quite pretty too, but Shelia didn't seem to have much to say. By coincidence, the four just happened to be single, so George invited the girls to meet them for dinner and maybe go dancing that night. Susan didn't want to speak for Shelia, but she acknowledged that they would meet them back there for dinner at six.

Shelia was a little put-off and said to Susan "what do you mean accepting a dinner invitation for both of us?"

"I didn't mean to do it without asking you, you haven't said anything so I supposed it would be okay. It's just a dinner date. We haven't committed to anything else yet."

"Okay then, let's see how it goes?"

After listening to lectures about government procedures all day, instead of dinner they wanted a drink, and at the conference center there were plenty of food choices too. Susan had already picked the one they would meet at. Susan was of course aware that this was just a casual dinner among medical colleagues. George arrived there early, even though it wasn't a date the girls went back to their rooms, and refreshed up. George had already told John the story of his other doctor friend named John from when he was in Africa.

They were not going to wait for the girls, so John ordered a couple of gin and tonics for him and George. *These are meant to help us unwind* George told himself. Then he said that to John, which brought a very good laugh. John was a little nervous, he thought that Shelia was cute and George agreed, but was not sure about her feelings for them. George then said "she appeared to be very bored with us."

"Well, we'll see if she is that way tonight?" John said.

The girls were walking toward them and John spotted Susan first noticing that she was a little bit taller than Shelia. When they were about fifteen feet away from the table, both men stood up, and pulled out a chair for each one of them. Somehow this might have been a scientific way of seeing who they would choose to sit with. Quickly, George thought as they were finding their seats *hum, I guess Shelia is interested in me instead?* Note, this wasn't a roundtable so, it offered itself to some form of discovery, and John wasn't so happy about that. Susan was taken aback, impressed, and flattered by their gentlemanly gesture.

John's mission was to call the waiter to get some drinks for the ladies. He seemed to try hard to impress both of them. George, on the other hand, didn't ignore them, but he didn't go out of his way to make small talk either. The waiter arrived and Susan asked Shelia if she knew what type of food she was going to order. Shelia seemed a little perplexed until she remembered that this was something her mom would do at dinner. Since Shelia had seafood and Susan wanted chicken, they both ordered a white wine, one sweet and the other drier.

Watching them work this out impressed George and he complimented both of them on their choices. They asked the waiter to return in about twenty minutes. John and George ordered another gin before dinner. There were some concise introductions except for John who seemed to want to jump right out there into the fray. The others were a little more reserved in talking about themselves. A consensus they mostly thought it was better to leave some conversation material for a later date.

It was an enjoyable dinner and they continued talking for two hours after the food was put away. The girls managed a few glasses of wine and the boys switched to some merlot which they shared a bottle. John talked about his childhood in Indiana and they seemed to enjoy listening to him talk. Maybe they were too tired to compete in his marathon ability to keep talking. It was around 10:30 when Shelia started to yawn. Susan looked at her and asked "are you getting tired doctor?"

This made her chuckle and say "you might say that." When in reality she was thinking *can this guy be any more boring?"* Her opinion of George was different.

It was the last night at the conference and everyone was packed and ready to travel home in the morning. They didn't finish their date. Okay then talking with the girls until shortly after 11 and that was only because the restaurant was closing, and it was too late for dancing. George and John finished the evening with a late night tonic and gin before retiring to bed. George had told John about his two buddies in Africa and how they would drink gin late into the evening. John liked the idea of carrying on that tradition.

They compared notes about the girls that they had met that week with the two from their date the previous night. The funny thing was that George would be polite and not say anything negative about either one of them and therefore not choosing one over the other. This was a talk in which both men helped each other to determine who should ask who for a phone number. Being a bit crafty, George suggested that they invite them to dinner again that night, and see where that would lead?

"George is a very handsome man" Susan said that morning while she and Shelia ate breakfast.

"Yes he is, but seems to be very confident about a lot of things."

"Well I don't know, just like you, he is a doctor. What do you think about John? Do you think he talks too much?"

"No, I think he was just excited to meet people I guess. I mean they are from Three Rivers, and that town is small."

"You're from Coldwater, so you should know."

They couldn't come to terms with who should go after whom. Instead they were content to see what will happen during dinner tonight. Although Shelia talked like she didn't care about George she did mention him a lot. The only time she mentioned John was when Susan did. She listened to Susan go on and on about not being able to pick one. Shelia thought *he seems like a challenge. Maybe that's what I need in my life, to meet a man who is not too easy to figure out? What am I saying? If I didn't catch on to what Jake was doing who knows if I would have any of daddy's money?*

Susan stopped talking, looked at her, and said "we better go to class."

Off they went and it just so happened that Shelia and John were in one of the classes together that day. He walked over to her and asked if she minded if he sat next to her, she, of course said she didn't mind him sitting there. During the twenty minute break they were able to talk with less pressure than on a date. During this time she was able to learn that George's wife and mother died and that he had just recently returned from a tour in Africa with Doctors without Borders. Also that John was a very nice man but not her type. Now George on the other hand was certainly a mystery that she wanted to unravel.

This day didn't turn out like anyone expected and that was good very good for two people that needed each other. Before meeting the boys, Shelia had discussed with Susan her conversations with John during their class break, and in that she asked her if it would be okay if she could sit next to George again tonight? Susan inquired why and Shelia informed her that the way John described George to her made her want to get to know him more.

Looking at the seriousness in Shelia's eyes Susan chuckled and said "I guess you being a doctor and all, I will acquiescence to your request," and then winked at her.

"Thank you, you are so gracious and comical too."

How things seem to move in the direction they were meant to go. Not only did George decide that he wanted to sit next to Shelia again, but after John talked with her during the break, he realized that she was only interested in George. That was fine with John, he felt that Susan was a lot more fun, and outgoing anyway. These doctors are so quick to assess any situation, then analyze it, and come up with the right solution.

Dinner that night was perfect for the couples, and I mean just that, couples. Not only were all four in agreement with who they wanted to be with, but they seemed to all hit it off so well that they went dancing later. During dinner Shelia opened up a little about being from New York City and about her dad's business that they sold. John and Susan seemed to be talking mostly to each other only. A few times they stepped outside to talk or kiss whichever you would prefer to call it.

George was an excellent dancer, which impressed the hell out of Shelia because Jake was a clod on the floor. That night he made her feel like a queen on the dance floor, swirling her around, lifting her hand properly, and looking her in the eyes with a sparkle that could only mean one thing. Dancing slowly around the floor her thoughts were *leaving Seattle, moving to Michigan, traveling to France, and now meeting this wonderful gentleman.* Truly a night to remember for one Shelia Ursula McCormick (she took back her maiden name).

Not wanting the night to end, John could only think about her. He had made plans with Susan to meet again when they both returned home. After all, they only lived fifty or so miles apart, what a small world we live in. Shelia and George did exchange phone numbers, but didn't make any plans to see each other again. Maybe they were not ready to move on in life after their first set of trials and testing. Either way they left a deep impression on each other.

While loading up that morning George looked several times for her. His traveling crew was ready to pull out, so he had to give up the search. One of the other doctors drove back and John talked with George about maybe seeing if they could double date again. He wanted to come back to Chicago for dinner, a show, and some dancing for a weekend. George thought that would be a great idea and to let him know when.

John took a nap and during the last thirty minutes of the drive George thought about her. *Is she the answer to my prayers? Am I being rewarded for my time in Africa with this beautiful woman? I'm not going to reject the good that comes to me. Lord knows I need to move on and have some semblance of a life.* The van then turned the corner, and they arrived at the car rental place where they all parked their cars for the week.

There were only two in the car when driving back home, so they had a lot to talk about, and it was terrific how neither of them was looking forward to meeting anybody before. But now they had dates and phone numbers to boot! Shelia was so swept up with George This man she thought was too confident a few nights ago was now the only one she could think about. Although they had exchanged phone numbers he still didn't ask to see her again, so she supposed that was that. *At least it wasn't a weekend fling* she assured herself of that.

She had enough of hearing Susan go on and on about how cute John could be and that they were meeting up again soon. When Shelia asked when and where? Susan didn't know, but they both promised to call each other to set it up. Susan pressed for Shelia to be assertive and call him and say hey or something. Shelia didn't like that idea for she thought it made her seem too eager. She drove to Susan's house and said goodbye and that they would have plenty to talk about at work on Monday.

CHAPTER 14

Was that to be it between George and Shelia? But that night was so memorable, it seemed like all their dreams were right there to be taken, and if only they could get past the fear of something terrible happening again! With friends like Susan and John, they could maybe find their way back to the lives they always wanted to have before.

Shelia was juggling her time at work, at home, with her mom and the children. She would now like to add George to that list, if only he called, she would like that very much. Having their weekends off was a blessing and at the same time it was a curse for these two positive people. Right now she was hopeful that the phone would ring.

The first day back was so uneventful. Steven found a friend a short distance from their home so he was gone all the time. Shelia's mom had Julie involved in some computer game that Shelia had no interest in learning.

Even if Shelia's family wanted to do something that day, it just wouldn't matter because though she loved them, she wanted to pursue a relationship with George. *What am I doing? I'm acting like a high school girl with a crush, but I am so lonely for some male company, except that my standards won't let me pick just any man.*

She was lost in her thoughts most of the day, and it didn't help her to gain the courage to call him. She had a glass of wine with her mom and some light conversation about the conference. She was very careful not to mention George because she knew that her mom would not let her procrastinate!

It's Sunday morning and they drove off to church. Her parents met in the cathedral in New York City after Sunday Mass. They attended the same Catholic school but her dad was several years older so they didn't get to know each other then. Today in the car and on the road travelling church, the kids had their Gameboy devices to play, but they were not to leave from the car with them, and that was the rule.

Her mom seemed to be lost in her thoughts *probably reminiscing about going to church with her husband* Shelia thought. With little time to drive, Shelia didn't want to indulge in those kinds of thoughts then because now she was taking in all the beautiful fall weather.

Bridges of Three Rivers

Shelia was looking forward to talking with Susan the following day at work. She had plans of asking her to lunch so they could talk privately. She only wanted to get through Sunday. This attitude that she had did not make her happy. While sitting in the backyard sipping some hot tea, her thoughts were *this is not who I am, I know I want to call him, but I don't have the courage. Am I still caught up in the old school ways of waiting for the man to make the move?* This went on for at least two hours before her cell phone rang! Trying to carefully place her tea down without spilling it wasn't easy, especially since the phone surprised her.

"Hello," she said.

"Shelia its Susan, I just got off the phone with John..."

There was a pause or maybe some interference with the cell. This silence seemed like an eternity for Shelia. Then it came back with Susan asking her.

"Well do you want to go?"

"Go where?" Shelia replied and then finished that with "the call was dropped. All I heard was that you just finished talking to John."

"Oh sorry, I didn't know. Well, John and I are going to Chicago for the weekend, two weeks from now, and he's planning everything. What I was asking you is that George would like you also to go."

"Then why didn't he call me?"

"I don't know; maybe he's as shy as you are about that?"

"When do I need to make my decision?"

She hesitated and said "Probably by the end of the week."

"Okay, I'll wait for George to ask me then."

Susan ended the call and then called John to tell him what Shelia had said.

Now with these two lovebirds working together towards a common goal, and that being helping their friends, this really brought them closer. John laughed when she told him what Shelia said about having George call her to ask her to go. There was a big laugh between them. He explained how methodically slow George worked on everything. This will probably push him to accelerate his dating schedule with her. Susan found it all amusing too, then she talked about how she would like to see John before the trip, and they made plans for Friday night.

"What do you mean I have to call her? Geez, I thought we were all past that stuff. I mean we've seen each other twice, so why can't she say yes, and then we will be with each other?"

John shook his head and said "man you just don't get it, do you? They like to be asked, to be let in on our plans, and of course treated like queens."

"Hum, I see your point. It would be nice to hear an invitation from me instead of a third party. Therefore I'll call her tonight after dinner and inquire about the possibility of her accompanying us to Chicago in two weeks."

"Now you're getting it."

Hours later he gathered up his courage and called her with a confidence that she had not seen in him before. As he talked with her, he asked how she was doing, and he made small talk that didn't last too long. For it was meant to get the air cleared of all updates since they last saw each other. She was patient and didn't mind waiting for him to get to the point. It wasn't that their conversation was boring, it wasn't, and she liked talking with him.

Once he was comfortable, he started telling her about how John asked if he would like to go to Chicago in two weeks. When John mentioned that Susan was going too he naturally assumed that Shelia was going also. Realizing that wasn't the case he then asked if she would like to go with them. Then very quickly after he said this he apologized to her. Not understanding why he did this she then asked him why?

His tone then said it all. He was calm, collective, and passionate when he said "I deeply desire that you join me for the weekend. I've thought about you constantly since our last night together."

Wow, she thought *he is a mystery, and I want to be with him for the weekend.* Then not realizing that now her lips were moving she said: "I wish I could see you sooner." She turned red-faced and thought *well at least he can't see how embarrassed I am.*

Bridges of Three Rivers

Then his answer made it all worthwhile when he said "I agree, let's do something this weekend. I live on a lake, maybe you can bring the kids, and I have lots of room for them to play and have fun."

Without any time for contemplating she said "sure, that sounds wonderful." Then she thought *he wants to meet my kids this early, that's impressive!*

The major goal for both George and Shelia was getting through the week. On Tuesday she had enough courage to text him to see how he was doing, but mostly to say hello. This made him feel good and started to bring back some old feelings he had years before. Texting is something that you do when you can't call, so when he replied to her text, he asked what time he should call her that night. She gave him a time, and when he was home, that was the first thing he did.

What's so interesting is how both attended Notre Dame's medical program during the same years, but never met. Then she went to Seattle while he lived close to home. She would get married while he spent time overseas. George informed Peter about meeting Shelia the previous week. Peter was so happy and thought that it was good to see his brother dating again. That didn't mean that there wasn't work to be done in getting Peter's wedding planned the following year in the spring.

Peter was a little jealous of his big brother since his girlfriend was nearby, while he had to travel to North Carolina. He was staying with George until he finished school to be a building contractor. George was excited for him and knew that once he was married, they were going to live in the Charlotte, North Carolina area. Until then he was there to help George with many projects that he planned while he was overseas.

That week, both men worked on getting the house ready for Saturday's visit by Shelia and her children. George and Shelia started texting every day, then talking on the phone after work. Susan would talk with her about meeting John on Friday night. Shelia asked her where they were going. She didn't have any idea, but he was going to drive to Coldwater, and pick her up at seven.

There's not much to do there in Coldwater Shelia thought as it was funny that John kept that as a surprise. She and George seemed to want to know what was going to happen. They started talking about the trip to Chicago in less than two weeks. Shelia wanted him to find out where they were going to stay, what restaurants they would eat, and where they were going for entertainment.

It's Saturday and Shelia was driving towards Three Rivers to George's home on the lake. He owned five acres with approximately three hundred feet of waterfront property. Since it was a family outing, she brought her mom, and also the children. Just in case George had two guest rooms ready for the evening. She pulled into the driveway, George and Peter headed to her car to unload the goodies that she and her mom baked. Her mom learned how to bake while living a few years in Paris, France before Shelia was born. They all made a beeline for the restrooms, and it was a good thing that George had two full and one half bathrooms.

"Let's all go outside." George motioned to them in the living room.

He had a nice big gazebo that he and Peter had put together a short while ago. With a big campfire and several chairs, then everyone took a break to warm up, and talk. They arrived shortly after lunch and their plan was to have dinner around six. When they sat around the fire to talk Shelia asked George about Africa. He told a few stories about their near-death escapes from the warlords and how they were there to help the indigenous people.

They all seemed interested in his stories, especially the ones about the warlords! George made them sound like pirates, only on land, and not very funny, unlike Johnny Deep. Daylight didn't come until six thirty and the time change hadn't happened yet either. They all enjoyed their time outdoors talking. Steven and Julie would get up, run down to the dock, and look at the water. Watching him Shelia thought *I could like this man, he seems very smart, and has a way with kids, but not superficial. I know I'm ready to try to finish raising my kids with a dad there for them.*

They all gathered around the two tables, one in the kitchen and the other in the dining room. George thought it would be nice if the kids could have their own table. This would keep them from being bored by adult conversations. With her mom there, George wanted to get to know the only living parent between them both. Peter talked about getting married in several months. Shelia's mom was very interested in hearing about their plans. Shelia and George sometimes talked about work, but mostly it was about the trip to Chicago the following week.

After drinking a couple glasses of wine, some homemade ice cream for the kids, all were getting tired. George informed Shelia that he had two guest rooms ready with both having queen sized beds. He let her know that with the wine, and the late hour it would be wise to spend the night. So they said goodnight to the others, grabbed their wine glasses, and headed out to the back porch where they spent the next hour sitting close on the swing.

After a toast of a gentle click of their glasses, she then leaned forward, and looked into his brown eyes, and thought, *I want to put my hands around the back of his head to pull him in for a kiss.* For not doing that, she caused him to pull back. Therefore, that night they were not going to enjoy a kiss. George said to himself, *for some reason, she is denying me? Well, it was worth a try, I won't try anything else unless she makes a move.* At this point they both thought that the other one wasn't interested in them.

He stood up and said "well, it was nice talking with you, and I know you need to get back home to attend church tomorrow, so I'll let you get some sleep."

Shelia was so hurt all she could think about was that he just rejected her. Her words came out very soft, and painfully she said "okay, thank you for letting us spend the night at your house."

They did not say another word during that evening and the misjudgment of this situation compounded with their fear only magnified any doubts they had about each other. For this reason, it certainly clouded their vision of what could have been. It was late, and they had said their brief goodnights that didn't amount to anything of encouragement. Seven hours later, they both woke up with a fog around them that hardened their hearts to the point of stress, which they both blamed on each other.

The kids were buzzing around the table in the kitchen while Peter helped Shelia's mom get breakfast ready. George woke up slowly and got dressed. He noticed the time and rushed downstairs hoping to see her. She was nowhere to be found and this helped his negative thoughts to put the proverbial nail in the coffin of their relationship. Peter said good morning to him but didn't notice the mood he was in. All this time she had dressed, made her bed, and just lay there with her nerves getting the best of her.

Tomorrow Susan's going to hear about this. Setting me up with this loser, she said to herself, and then quietly cried again. Whatever was going on downstairs didn't bother her, since she couldn't go, and let him see that she had been crying. If he did and he was to ask, she had made up in her mind to tell him it must be allergies. So, she didn't want breakfast and then waited until they started to call for her. She walked down the stairs and she looked at Peter for she couldn't look at George at least not for that moment. She acknowledged Peter and then ordered the kids to load up their luggage in the car because they needed to get back home to get ready for church.

They went out the door while he just stood there barely waving goodbye. With his hand up in the air waving he thought about how perfect he thought they were, only to have her reject him. Negative thoughts raced in his head, *maybe she's gay, and doesn't like men? Who knows this day and age what women like.* Whatever his mind was thinking, his heart was hurt. He wished she could be the one, and again he had it all planned out. Now, he didn't have the heart ever to try and make any plans in life, only to have them fail.

I seem to be on the lonely road of life, was her thought driving towards Three Rivers. Since she didn't want to be in a bad mood, she tried to pull herself up.

She noticed the beautiful countryside and asked the kids what they thought of the area. Both said it was nice and told her how much they liked the house by the lake. Trying to keep up her appearance she agreed and then started to talk about their trip to France. This confused the kids, but being young they quickly pushed that question aside, and instead asked her when they were going back to visit George and Peter.

"I don't know kids he is a very busy man."

Julie said "Mr. Peter is very nice too. We liked it when he took us out on the lake in his boat."

Steven chimed in "yea, that was fun, and he told me he would teach me how to fish."

Shelia and her mom sat there in the front seat listening to the kids talk about how much they liked the place. She had a little lump in her thought, and she held back some tears, knowing that they probably wouldn't go back there again.

CHAPTER 15

Stubborn, bullheaded, there are many names for it, but what we have here is a failure to communicate. I think I've heard that many years ago in a Paul Newman movie. It's been three months since that Saturday at his home, and they didn't go to Chicago the following weekend. Both came up with some lame excuse for not being able to go. Life certainly wasn't any better for Shelia or George, and after three months, the pressure from their friends had finally stopped. They were now free to be over the thought of ever finding someone.

George was lost in his work thinking about an old friend. He contacted his engineer friend Calvin who was in Africa. Calvin had finished up his tour a couple of months before and was now at home in Chicago. Calvin went to college for mechanical engineering with a minor in medical devices. He was excited when he talked with George about the new knee implants they had discussed and wanted to work with him on developing some new ideas. They made plans to meet in Chicago for the weekend. George had also wanted to go up there for a show.

He asked Peter if he would like to accompany him, but he was flying to North Carolina to spend some time with his fiancé, or as he called her his "bride to be." It was not a long drive, and the weather was a little bit cold, but sunny so the roads should be alright. During the drive, his thoughts were on Shelia and what had happened at his house. *Sure, I wish things could have worked out for us, she was a nice girl.* His mind drifted off into other areas, just recalling Christa and how perfect she was for him. Before he knew it his eyes were filled with tears from the sadness of losing her.

He was spending the night at Calvin's, so as he turned off the interstate, and then turned toward the road to Calvin's he could see the Marriott in the distance. Although he wasn't staying there that night, it brought him back to those memories of meeting Shelia a few months ago, and this caused him to say to himself *great job George Esperanza you sure messed that one up.* After saying that, he smacked the steering wheel and grunted!

Before the conference in Chicago, Shelia didn't know Susan that much, but since then they had become good friends. Especially after she had stopped bugging her about George, although sometimes she wished she

Bridges of Three Rivers

would. That day at work was the last day before the Christmas holiday, and she brought something that her mom helped her make. It was an old family fruit cake recipe that was guaranteed to be a favorite. Shelia wanted to do this to take her mind off you know who and it helped.

The chief doctor of their practice mentioned to his wife about "shaking up the party" some two weeks in advance. When she heard that, the first thing she thought of was *why not make it bigger by inviting some of the other practices in the area to attend?* She suggested this to her husband, and he liked the idea, but they would need a larger place to hold it. Her husband gave it to her to handle, and she planned big. The first thing was to find a few places to hold it there at least a week before the event. That way the invitations could have a week to go out and RSVP. She included around thirty practices and clinics in the South Bend and Elkhart area.

There is nothing like spending time with an old friend. George and Calvin shared a friendship like the one military personnel do. When you share a tent in the desert, work with limited supplies to help poverty-stricken people, and flee from bandits for almost two years. I guess you would be very close indeed in these situations. The weekend plan was to hang out and get caught up. Also, Calvin wanted some advice from George of places that he could apply for an engineering position in the medical field. George wanted to show him some new designs of knee replacement parts he had sketched up.

On the outskirts of Chicago were many suburbs, Calvin lived in one called Rolling Meadows. This was next to Schaumburg which is where George went before for a medical conference. For some reason after arriving at Calvin's place, he dropped off his clothes, made a bathroom stop, had a glass of tea, reminisced with Calvin, and then was ready to go someplace for lunch.

He Set his tea glass down, and then said to Calvin while stretching "I have a place that I want us to go for lunch."

"Okay, when do you want to leave?"

George said "how about in thirty minutes?"

George wanted to go to a local Pizza place named California Pizza Kitchen. When he was in the Air Force stationed in California, he would go there with some of his comrades. That's what he told Calvin, but that was many years back, and the real reason why he wanted to go there was because that's the last place he had dinner with Shelia during their time in Chicago. While waiting for their meal, he felt the need to talk to an old friend about his predicament with Shelia.

Calvin gave him some good advice during their lunch. He told Calvin about how he leaned over to kiss her, and she seemed to reject him. Calvin asked him, "How did she reject you?" The answer he gave was very vague in that he supposed that she rejected him, but he wasn't sure, all he knew was that she didn't make a move to meet him in the middle.

That's when Calvin laid it out to him and said "Let me get this straight. You met her on a business trip here in Schaumburg. Nothing really happened at first, but the last night you went out again, and there was something there. Before she could leave you didn't make any plans with her. Luckily your friend was with her friend and asked you to come back here for a weekend. She required you to ask her to go, and in conjunction with that you invited her to your house for the weekend before Chicago." He then looked at George.

"Okay that's all correct, so what's your point?"

"My point is; you met a very nice lady, one that you could fall in love with. She comes to your home, spends the night, and you think she's rejecting you because when you tried to kiss her, she didn't maul you with her lips?"

"Damn, you engineers know how to figure things out."

"Thanks, other than all that, what do you want to do?"

George felt more courage in him and said: "I want to fall in love with her."

He put that thought in his front pocket and decided to enjoy the weekend with his friend. That weekend was about seven days before Christmas so since the traffic in the malls was horrendous, instead they went out on Lake Michigan, and braved the cold weather. The cold weather was something they didn't have when they were in Africa because that place was hot! Spending time with Calvin was great! Both talked a lot about things that were happening. George shared some names of several medical companies, especially in the Warsaw, Indiana area.

At the Christmas party, there were over a hundred people, mostly doctors. Mingling around she wondered if he would be there and thought, *but then again what did it matter. He didn't want anything to do with me anyway.* An hour or so later she spotted John and Susan, they were so much in love, and she wondered if there wasn't an announcement coming soon. She said "hello" trying not to ask where George was. She waited to hear that news from them.

"Shelia, come over here" Susan waved to her while John was getting them another drink.

She noticed her waving and moved around, then walked towards her carefully looking to see if she could also spot George. With John still holding their drinks, Susan moved out to greet her with a hug. Laughing from this because Shelia was a little ticklish and that Susan loved to show affection. *Maybe I should be more like her* was her thought as she embraced her. John just stood there smiling, holding their drinks, and watching them.

"So, how do you two like the party so far?" Shelia asked acknowledging both of them.

John said "well, it's pretty good, but I wish George would have made it."

"Oh, so he didn't then?" Once she said that she thought *great, now they will start back into their nagging of "why don't you call or text him, I'm sure he wants to hear from you?" Right, then why doesn't he do it? Furthermore love is two-way street and it has to be reciprocated.*

For some unknown reason, they just smiled at her, and said "see you later" then turned and left.

As they walked away, she could barely hear John say to Susan "I guess she doesn't know that he is going to Chicago for the weekend."

"No, apparently not" Susan answered him.

What a great friend Calvin was! That evening they had plans to see a show at the Fox Theater. Seeing that George had come alone, Calvin was going to remedy that. He excused himself for about an hour and retired to his bedroom where he shut the door. George was perplexed, but thought that Calvin needed to make a private phone call. What Calvin did was to call his girlfriend and asked if she might have a friend that would like to go out that night? She happened to have one that needed something to take her mind off a current experience.

At first, George was against it, but Calvin convinced him that it was only dinner, and a show date, nothing long term. *You know, I should try to be a little more outgoing, and this is a perfect example of doing just that.* He finished that thought and said "awesome idea, I knew you were my best friend for a reason."

Calvin was very happy because after working with this man in the rough environment of Africa and seeing him help so many people, doing something for him was a joy. Being Calvin, he only replied, "it was nothing. You deserve the best in all things."

They had a fantastic time at this Italian restaurant that Calvin swore by. Later, they went to the station to take a train into the city. His date was a very shy and sweet girl, they didn't hit it off, but they enjoyed each other's company. All the while George was his polite, gentlemanly self, his thoughts were on Shelia, and how he wanted another chance. *Maybe, just maybe we can see each other again. There is so much I would love to share with her.*

George and Shelia both spent the Christmas season thinking about each other. They had one thought in common, and that was a strong desire to be with one another. If not for the dark cloud of fear and ignorance, they could be able to move on with their purpose of being together. She just checked every box she could come up with on everything about him. On the other hand, her strength of character, kindness, and being a single mother like his mom. This really spoke to his heart. It's not that he wasn't physically attracted to her. He was very much attracted to her in every way. Why wouldn't he be "she was a knock-out" is what he told Peter, and Peter couldn't agree more.

CHAPTER 16

What George liked to do was to always help a friend. After spending more time with Calvin going over his designs of some new knee replacements, they came to many conclusions about what needed to be done to bring them to the market. George provided the ideas to Calvin, who took them, created models on the computer, and then performed the stress and kinematic studies. However in doing this Calvin was not able to determine if the motions that were the required standards would work, but they were pretty close, so with some minor adjustments he was able to finalize them, and make an early prototype using his 3D printer.

George not only invited him to his home, but the plan they came up with was for him to stay until Wednesday. Before Calvin arrived, George had gathered the data that they put together then showed it to a few doctors and engineers in the area. With most of them showing a great interest. This prompted George to schedule some meetings. These places were local, mostly in South Bend, and Warsaw. At first George talked with Calvin about interviewing with some of these companies and that's when a thought occurred to him. One thought where he asked Calvin if now wouldn't be more advantageous time to start their advanced engineering company.

Calvin liked that idea but wondered if they had enough capital for funding, plus he would need to move closer, and needed a source of income for himself. As they bantered these ideas and restrictions around a plan was had. That plan entailed Calvin moving in with George, especially since Peter would be leaving in less than a few months anyway. Also, they were going to patent their new designs, and then sell them to the knee replacement companies.

In their first meeting they were in South Bend with several D.O.'s, mostly the ones that specialized in knees, and hip replacements. This meeting was very beneficial in that they gained some needed suggestions as well as approvals from these front-line doctors. Having been pleased with their progress that day, they went out that night, and celebrated it over their favorite drink of gin and tonic.

The next two days there were meetings in Warsaw with the three big orthopedic manufacturing companies. Some were so impressed with Calvin that they wanted to hire him. George had it planned already to thank them and inform them that Calvin was under contract at that time. These companies also provided a few suggestions, some of these suggestions were more so to help them get FDA approval, and the ease of manufacturing processes. George said to his business partner "the next step is FDA approval. Then off to selling our designs!"

She was disappointed since she didn't even have a chance to see him again, now back in her old world of working, in which it only involved her dedication to taking care of her patients. Sometimes she wished her dad was around to talk to, but then again she thought *what would he know? He was taken in by that snake of a husband, Jake.* Even thinking about that made her sad to a point where she used the words snake and Jake in the same sentence. That seemed to bring a big laugh inside her. This day she decided to give up on ever seeing George again. She thought he was not a worthwhile distraction in her life.

Only then she needed to formalize her plan and that was of course a joke. Shelia couldn't make a plan even if she were forced to. With that said she wanted nothing more than to find a group of people to engage with. She was still friends with Susan, *but Shelia didn't want to hang out with me* is what Susan thought. Shelia was feeling sad and wanted to make it right, but all the while knew that hanging out with Susan outside working hours could only risk her seeing George again. She hadn't heard from him for so long thus she didn't think she wanted that problem.

Life with her mom was good and Christmas was also good for the kids. Not that they ever did without, but without the conflicts of Jake back in Seattle it made things much more pleasurable. There was plenty of snow in Coldwater and with it led to them traveling to the school to snowboard down the hills. They were having fun as a family and with her mom there with her to watch the kids enjoy themselves. Shelia was happy, she produced a half happy smile for all of them to see, and even went down the hill once or twice.

A couple of doctors that she met at the Christmas party seemed to be interested in dating her. She gave them her number, but she didn't give them any promises. With New Year's Eve on the way, she wondered if she would celebrate at home with the family or maybe go with some of her colleagues to the Holiday Inn in South Bend. All the while Susan and John were still working behind the scenes to reunite them. Susan just needed to get her to go out with her and her other colleagues to celebrate that night.

At work with John, George was having lunch with him that day, and it being the last day of the year. For John to convince him to attend a New Year's Eve party that night wouldn't be easy. Nevertheless, John would try convincing him since he wasn't going to let George miss the opportunity, not after listening to him after his visit to Chicago. This was what he would remind him of every time George would say he couldn't attend. The one thing for sure is that John couldn't guarantee that she would be there. Although he informed him that she had attended the Christmas party.

Their conversation during lunch went like this, John said "my friend you need to get out more."

George then responded with "yes, you are correct, I've been lonely much too long."

"Okay then, are you going to the party tonight?"

"I don't know. Is there any good reason I should go?"

That's when John was firm with him "listen you can't keep remembering what might have been for the rest of your life. You need to give her a chance, you said yourself that you thought she might be the one."

"I know John, you are right. Thanks, I will see you there tonight."

"Awesome, now let's eat lunch!"

He finished his afternoon appointments and then went back home to let his brother know that he would attend the party that night. On the drive home he imagined what was going to happen there at the party;

There she'll be so pretty in a blue open shoulder cut dress, maybe in those four-inch heels. When I see her, I'll greet her with "you look so lovely tonight." I'll ask her if she would like a drink and she'll say "yes, thank you." As I will be returning she'll smile at me, I'll then hand her the drink, and tell her how sorry I am for whatever happened at my home. This will bring on a smile and then she'll try to say it was her fault. I will hold her hands and tell her it doesn't matter because being without her isn't worth it. Then I'll dance with her until the countdown begins. We will do the countdown together, drink some champagne, and give each other a very passionate kiss. I will hold her so tight and tell her that I don't want to be without her anymore. She will look me in the eyes with happy tears and agree to stay in touch.

This night was the night for getting their relationship back on track. Let's hope that George was right in predicting how the evening would go down. He arrived a little late, but he had not planned that, he wanted to be there early, but had to perform some extra medical work on his last operation. The surgery went well except there was some infection that wasn't found in the pre-surgery check-up. This is not terrible and doesn't happen that often. What was needed was to add some medicated bone cement to the stem to clear the infection.

Shelia was already there with Susan and John to take in the New Year. John told her that he would be there soon. He let her know that being late wasn't his plan because he was finishing up with a patient. After George was done it was 7:45, he brought his suit, changed into it, and left at 8:30. Traffic wasn't too bad, just a little heavy, so what normally took thirty minutes was now forty-five. Every minute was worth it knowing that he would see her that night after waiting nearly half a year! It was close to 9:30 when he arrived.

Then when he entered the door, Shelia stood there in her blue dress with those four-inch heels on, she looked at him walking in, and that old Carly Simon song started in her head. In her head she heard *you walked into the party like you were walking onto a yacht. Your hat strategically dipped below one eye... enough of that* she thought *he's not even wearing a hat.* He walked up to her and said: "you look so lovely tonight." She smiled and then he asked her "would you like a drink?"

"Yes, thank you" she replied with a smile.

George returned and gave her the drink where she then gave him another smile.

"I'm so sorry for what happened at my house."

With a smile, she said, "no it was my fault."

He then took both of her hands, looked her in the eyes, and said "it doesn't matter being without you isn't worth it."

Then he took her to the dance floor, where they spent most of the next two hours dancing, with only several breaks after a few songs each time. Once 11:55 had arrived, they both grabbed a glass of champagne, and waited together for the countdown. Then they heard "*ten nine eight seven six five four three two one*

Bridges of Three Rivers

HAPPY NEW YEAR!" Looking into each other's eyes they embraced for a long hug and then rolled that into a very long passionate kiss.

George moved back and said "I don't ever want to be without you again."

Her face had happy tears rolling down her cheeks, and she said "I want to see and talk to you every night and visit on the weekends."

With the biggest smile he could give her, he said "I would like that very much, now what are you doing after the party?"

When they left the party, they didn't go home that night. They didn't go far at all because there were still some rooms available at the Holiday Inn. There was even a suite with a whirlpool Jacuzzi! They brought a bottle of champagne up with them and a lot of pent-up romance. Their date night was one night to remember for many years. Romance goes a long way when it's with the one you want to spend the rest of your life with. Maybe they weren't ready to get married, but they felt they were with the right one. All they needed now was time to date and get to know each other better.

With a late breakfast the next morning, that was so wonderful, George thought *even the orange juice tastes better today. Yes, that's silly, but I feel she makes everything in my life better.* The conversations were the best they've ever had, and they even mentioned what they thought the problem was at his home several months earlier. This enlisted great laughter because they both realized that it was just a misunderstanding, and so stupid.

CHAPTER 17

With a new look on life Shelia was now ready to give men another try. This, of course, was always her plan since moving from Seattle. Only now she thought of it as going back to an old way of life. That day she was so happy that reconnecting with Jenny seemed like the thing to do. Jenny was very good at helping her see the big picture in what was happening at the time. The move to the Midwest was one that Jenny said would be her chance to go back to dating men.

She was beaming with light willing to try again especially after the New Year's Eve party. She was so upbeat to be talking with George again. One thing that was so important to her was that after Jake, Jenny, and all the years of trying to make a relationship happen, this man seemed to be what she had been looking for all along. They planned to meet that Saturday with her mom and the kids at his house. He instructed her that they would need to pack for a night there.

Bridges of Three Rivers

The kids were so excited about the prospect of having another weekend at the lake. Julie invited a girlfriend to come with her. Her mom approved as long as her parents knew they were going to the lake. With Peter still there Steven wished they could do some fishing, but the lake was frozen so ice fishing was all they could do. Steven enjoyed being in a boat on the lake with Peter, but instead they would go ice fishing. Getting them up early for school was never that easy! Shelia noticed that they were awake and knocking on her door. Rolling over and putting her feet on the floor Shelia said "geez, you'd think it was Christmas!"

In the car they were loaded for the weekend. Steven had his iPod listening to music while Julie and her friend Stacy just laughed and giggled. The front seat was quiet, Shelia was thinking about seeing him again, this feeling was so good, yet somehow brought about a fear she couldn't explain. Looking at her daughter her only child, Shelia's mom was now content that she would be fine in life. She wanted to say something to her, but seeing her look so happy, there was no good reason to disturb her.

They arrived a little early, but George had no problem with that, he had been ready over an hour earlier. When she pulled in, the kids were so excited that she wasn't sure if they could even wait for the car to stop. "Kids, kids, settle down. Steven put that seatbelt back on, you do not unbuckle until the car is parked" Shelia didn't yell this, but since she wanted them to hear, her voice was a bit high. On opening her door, George was right there to help her out. Before she had parked, he had already asked Peter if he would mind taking care of her mom.

She felt somehow lucky her children acted very respectful to other people. This probably came from her example at home, a way that she had learned from her mom. In addition, Jenny was a very respectful girl. So lastly the fact that they were too young to be influenced by Jake was a blessing. George was so taken aback by their mindfulness and energy to have fun.

Lunch was in an hour and so all were asked to contribute. George worked at preparing the salad when he called up Shelia to help with cutting up the vegetables. This scene was like any romantic movie out there even when these two lovebirds sliced the French bread together. Her mom took the girls, had them put ice in the drinks, and helped her mix the Kool Aide. Peter had his buddy Steven with him on the grill cooking burgers and hot dogs. George had an industrial stove that had a gas grill in the middle.

They spent the night in the house which didn't make a big difference since it was cold outside. Peter and Steven had brought back a few fish from their day of ice fishing. Peter taught him how to clean and fillet them in the kitchen. A movie was playing in the living room for the girls, and grandma brought some knitting to do. With big smiles on their faces, Shelia and George looked at each other with the expression of mischief, but the trouble they were going to get into tonight was only good.

He had it planned for a few days knowing his room was going to be their final destination that night. It was now time for the plan to start. It wasn't that he didn't want to plan everything he enjoyed spontaneity when it suited his purpose. Watching their family members go to their areas for the evening, he took hold of her hand in a symbolic gesture to say *you are with me tonight,* and she didn't mind that gesture one bit.

They were alone now ready to take the pleasures of the night, which they had worked for, and looked forward to all week long. Attached to his room was a lovely study area that also doubled as a nice sitting room if a couple of things were moved around. With a hold of her hand, he then moved her with him to the left, and walked upstairs. Pushing his bedroom door wide open, she thought *wow he's moving fast tonight!* With that thought in her mind, she still didn't resist even once.

Walking past the bed that had candles lit around it he took her towards the window. Without any idea what he was doing, she wanted to speak to him, but she couldn't think of any words to say. There was another door in his room? She was confused as her thoughts were *is he taking me to his bathroom?* Then with her second part of that thought, she chuckled as she thought *his closet.* Being quiet all this time he asked softly "what's so funny?"

Once they walked through the doorway, she answered him "nothing really, I thought you might be taking me into your bathroom or closet."

Talk about bringing a combined, coordinated laugh between them. They had to hug each other to settle down. Their connection with this energy that night was so powerful. He showed her where they were to sit and there was the love seat that Peter had helped him bring upstairs. With her in the seat, he went over to a mini-fridge and brought out a plate of *hors d'oevres.* She smiled and said "Sweetheart you are the perfect host tonight."

"Hah, that's not all there is." He then turned around and walked back to the fridge and grabbed a bottle of an expensive white wine.

Feeling very content, she said, "Mr. Esperanza, you are the perfect host, sir."

They sat there on the very cozy couch, sipping wine, slicing cheese, and enjoying their *hors d'oevres.* It was a perfect night looking over at the lake, the moon shining brightly, and the stars so bright. Sitting there quietly and taking it all in. It all felt so nice holding hands and just sitting there together.

His thoughts started to go in a direction that he didn't like, *will she not make the move that I think she should, and will I become upset feeling that I've been rejected.* Releasing her hand he then told himself *I refuse to allow negativity to take me in this direction again. What is happening here is a beautiful thing therefore I'm going to carry on in this direction.* The time it took between releasing her hand and putting his arm around her took around five seconds!

Wonderful was what she thought with his arm around her, looking out the window over the lake she made sure to breathe in this magical air that night. *I was so stupid to think he rejected me before. Now how do I make sure we don't have any misunderstandings again?* Thinking about the bad that can happen again really wasn't helping her mood that night. It would take time for their love to grow stronger, and it certainly needed to do just that.

When they were finished drinking the wine, they talked about sharing their dreams together and doing lots of kissing. It was time for them to leave, which they did. They left that room but didn't leave his bedroom until late in the morning. He was so gentle with her, caring, loving, and attentive to her needs.

Back In the lake house with his brother Peter. George was very happy thinking about his next visit with her. They had now dated for a few months, and Peter was finishing up his school, he only had two weeks to go. This was sad news for George because he knew that Peter was then moving back to North Carolina to get ready for his wedding in less than two months. George had already asked Shelia if she would attend Peter's wedding in which she answered in the affirmative. Now he needed to make plans to fly her and the kids down there, but her mom wasn't up to flying back in one day, so she stayed at home in Coldwater.

Flying wasn't anything new for the kids, but they had never been to a wedding before. With Peter's fiancé making most of the arrangements their court was mostly set. All Peter had to do was to choose his best man, which was easy for him because it was to be his brother. His court was made up of two of his best friends from the Air Force and two friends from high school. Instead of taking a plane to Chicago, they decided to take the train from South Bend to Chicago.

Shelia just allowed George to make all the plans, even though they had been dating for several months, she didn't want to tell him about the money she had from selling her daddy's business.

They took a direct flight to Raleigh to stay one night and then drove to a little lake outside of Southern Pines for the wedding. She was aware of the next day's agenda, which also included a late flight from Raleigh on that day too. On the plane her thoughts were *a wedding is a big event to spark certain feelings. Maybe he'll get some inspiration about our future. Oh well, I guess I can dream about that day.*

Losing her again was anathema to him, for he felt strongly about sharing the rest of his life with her.

Bridges of Three Rivers

On one of their dates, she told him her story about her first husband Jake, and how she had nicknamed him snake. In telling the story she tried not to change it too much, but she didn't altogether tell him the entire story. In talking with George, she was careful not to tell him about the money she had, and to her, he didn't seem to care about money anyway.

On landing, in Raleigh, she and George worked like a married couple getting their children ready and off the plane. The stewards and flight attendants even addressed them as a married couple when ordering drinks.

They spent the night at the airport's Hyatt, and there was no need to get the car until morning. All their needs were met at the airport for that evening. To keep things normal George booked two rooms, one with two queen sized beds for him and Steven, while the other was a king sized bed for Julie and Shelia.

They had a good night's sleep and then in the morning they had breakfast at the Inn. While the girls got dressed, George took Steven to the rental counter to get the car. The plan was to meet the girls downstairs, then drive to the lake near Southern Pines for Peter's garden wedding. It was a beautiful June day in North Carolina and this was a drive to remember for a very special day for four people!

Bridges of Three Rivers

Heart-stopping, maybe not, after all, that sounds deadly, but isn't "drop dead" a fatal term too? Let's say her dress was amazingly perfect for this special day. She was so beautifully appealing, walking with her dad skillfully down the path of rose petals to meet her future husband. Peter stood there thinking about what a lucky man he is. She was the light in his eyes, the one who made him better, and his queen!

The wind blew softly, the sky couldn't have been bluer, birds sang love songs, and Peter longed for this day. The minister said those special words, then asked them the questions of their intentions to each other, and if they were willing to commit them in their lives. Peter turned to George, his best man and asked for the ring. He carefully took it, placed it on her ring finger, and she gave her answer of "I do."

She then received his ring from her bridesmaid, slid it on his finger, then smiled at him, and he also said "I do."

They danced at the reception, but once Peter was ready to go on the honeymoon, they didn't stay much longer. After they left George and Shelia packed the kids in the car and then drove to the Raleigh airport for their flight back to Chicago, got onto a train to South Bend, and drove home to the lake where they were going to spend the night. No wonder Shelia's mom didn't want to go to the wedding. They made it back home safely, but that weekend's excitement wasn't over yet.

CHAPTER 18

They were too tired to do anything that morning and fortunately it was Sunday. He and Shelia had made plans to spend the day there on the lake house together. Lying with her next to him his thoughts were; *this is what I've longed for all of my life, a beautiful wife, two sweet children, and a profession that I love, and this house on a lake in the area where I grew up.* She started to wake up when the sunlight broke through the curtains. He looked at her from behind, then she turned around, reached forward, grabbed his head, and gave him a sweet morning kiss. He smiled at her, then looked into her green eyes and said "I love you."

It was not the first time he had said this, but for some reason, she felt the power of those words from his lips. Then she put her hands on his round shoulders and said "I love you so much, George."

While getting up slowly he waited in the bed for her to finish in the bathroom. Laying there his thoughts continued with; *she said she loves me and I think those words were filled with a passion that I hadn't noticed in her before. I believe the time is right to take this relationship to the next level.* With the bathroom ready for him, he then kissed her as he passed on his way to the door. When he finished, she was already dressed so he told her that he would meet her downstairs. After she had left the room, he located her surprise then got dressed, and headed down the stairs.

The kids sat down waiting for breakfast while they prepared it for them. Their minds were both racing with the same visions of this being an ongoing occurrence together. George had thought about this for weeks and he had previously asked Peter question after question about how that scene would go down. Afterwards they both agreed that this would be the best time and place to do it. Steven and Julie were both so sweet and appreciative of how great the food was. George finished first, stood up, and collected the dishes.

When he returned, he looked at her right in the eyes, then scanned over to the kids, and said to them "I have something special to ask your mom."

Steven then asked "do you want us to leave?"

Laughing a little, he said "no, son I want you, and your sister here to hear this."

Then walking over to where she sat, he said "Shelia."

With a nervous voice, she said "yes George."

Before she could finish saying his name he was already down on one knee. He then reached into his pocket and pulled out a little jewelry box. She put her hand over her mouth, and her tears started to drop. Quickly knowing what he was going to say, her thoughts were; *to moisten my mouth, I don't want to have anything impede my answer.* Then he asked her, "Shelia Ursula McCormick (she took back her maiden name) will you marry me?"

Then she didn't say what she thought she was going to say, and instead she said "absolutely I will!"

He then placed this gorgeous three diamond engagement ring on her finger. He and Peter didn't think it would be fair to create a competition between them for their mom's ring to put on their bride's finger. That ring had been put in a safe place as a family treasure for many generations to admire.

The kids were ecstatic when she said "absolutely I will." Right then they knew their lives were about to change, not that their lives were terrible, but with George as their dad, it would undoubtedly be for the better.

He did not want to disturb his brother on his honeymoon in England. Peter's new wife had always wanted to go there because of the stories that her parents would tell her. She was born years after they were stationed there. Spending time at Fort Bragg was the only place she'd ever lived. Her dad joked with her about meeting an airman and not a soldier, but secretly he couldn't be any happier. George sent him a text because he had promised to let him know her answer. Luckily she had a spa treatment that day, so Peter played some golf, and decided to call George instead of text him back.

The feelings that George had weren't there since Christa was pregnant with their first child. They were a welcomed feeling, for he liked feeling this way with love, and promise in his heart. Wishing that Peter would have chosen his lake house to have the ceremony on, but her parents just had too many people to attend, so logistically it wouldn't work. However, Shelia was more than happy to have their wedding there, the kids loved the place, and they were going to live there after the wedding. Steven and Julie were both in a private school, so it didn't matter where they lived in the area.

Shelia had a concern about her family's money, and talking with her mom, she gained some enlightenment. Their conversation could have escalated into a full-blown argument if it weren't for her mom's inability to use that level of energy. Shelia was set on having a prenuptial agreement with him, but her mom thought that this would only cause her doubts to grow. It wasn't until her mom calmly and skillfully created a metaphorical story for her to envision the problem. Shelia changed her mind per this conversation with her very wise mother.

Planning the wedding would take her down a different road. She had a great feeling about this man being her final companion in life. Therefore her thoughts were; *okay I've been married before and so has he, I want to change things up, and not having a church wedding is the first thing to change.* With these thoughts flowing so fast, she decided to start writing them down. Then be able to put them together into a most different and beautiful wedding plan later. Even though they felt they were ready to tie the knot again, they still wanted to wait until May of the following year, and this gave her almost a year to plan.

Putting aside the doubts of feeling the need for a prenuptial freed her up to spend more money on the wedding. She still wasn't ready to reveal her family's wealth yet nor did she have a time set to do that. Spending money on their wedding or honeymoon was something she had no problem with. I think that is when George would realize that she was loaded.

Secrets are not always kept for a long time, and the closer two people are, the harder it is to keep them. Three months after Peter's wedding and their announcement, these two were going strong. One day George went fishing on the lake with Steven in his boat since the weather was not too cold, and supposedly the fish were biting. Steven had never been told the story of his grandpa having many businesses and lots of money. However, he had heard his mom talk with his grandma recently about having a lot of money to spend on their honeymoon.

In the boat, they talked about school, girls, and fishing. They were having a great time and even mentioned how they wished Peter could be there with them. Steven liked calling him Uncle Peter, even though George and his mom weren't married yet. Making small talk, George jokingly asked him if his mom mentioned where their honeymoon was going to be. That's when Steven said "I don't know where, but I know she told grandma that she planned on spending a lot of the family's money on it."

He then told Steven, "I'm sure it will be a nice place. I like not knowing, I've been to many places, but very few were for a vacation."

Somehow what Steven told George didn't seem that important to even think about, but on one of their dates it came up. George wanted that night to be romantic; not two people who were in love working, and planning their future. What he was after was, dinner once a week, followed by dancing or a movie, and every second or third week to spend the weekend in the city, preferably Chicago. This was one of those weekends in the big city, and they were in their room talking about the wedding. Clandestinely he asked her where they were going for the honeymoon now that he was aware that she planned on spending a lot of money, and right then something triggered in her.

"How did you know that?" She asked.

"Know what?"

"That my family had money."

Not knowing what she was exactly talking about, he tried to remember where he had heard about the honeymoon being expensive. For some reason, he felt that telling her who said this to him would only get that person in trouble, and that didn't seem right at all. He quickly thought; *I will tell her that I can't remember if I had heard something or if it was just learned from our conversations.* Forgetting all of that, he blurted out "I can't tell you that."

That was a place she didn't want to go back to, but keeping her secret was creating a problem, and she could see that. Learning to stop and think about the situation was a promise that she had made after they started dating again. In her thoughts she was telling herself; *don't go there, don't become suspicious of him, he hasn't given you a reason to do that. Tell him that's okay, but we shouldn't keep secrets.* Instead of clear thinking, his words seemed to stir up something that she didn't want to say. "So, you're wondering about my money."

That wasn't said as a question, it was directed at him as a statement. Remember he knows nothing about what happened with Jake. In his mind his thoughts were; *why is she trying to hurt me? What did I say that was so wrong? I'm thankful that I didn't just lash out, and tell her that I don't give a damn about her money. Which before today I didn't even know she had?* He had never been intentionally hurt before from another relationship, and this left George with a little more room in his heart to withstand these arrows that she was shooting at him.

All he could say was "I'm not concerned about any money you might have. I never knew you had any money until now, and I have no idea how much you have."

This is where she shouldn't have said anything, at least not when she said "well, George my money is my money, I think we need to get that straight from the beginning."

This man lost his dad when he was a toddler, worked hard on the farm to help his mom, served in the Air Force as a pararescue airman; he put himself through medical school, lost his first true love in a road accident, and then spent two years in a hell hole helping poor people survive in Africa. Do you think he was for one minute concerned about her damn money? Before he could speak, he said to himself *I don't know if this is worth it?*

Without a word, he turned around, packed his suitcase, looked at her and said: "I'm sure you can make your way back home."

What have I done? Was all she could think. *Is he another Jake, of course not? So then why am I so stupid?* She laughed a little bit through her tears and thought; *that was a rhetorical question. Wasn't it?* She wasn't mad that he left her; in fact, he had every right to do that. So then why did she destroy what they had, and what was the status of their wedding the following year? After crying and wishing she could have that time back to explain to him what Jake had tried to do so many years ago, she said to herself; *he probably won't take my phone call, so I'll send him a text and apologize.* In the text she wrote "George, I'm so sorry, I beg you to let me explain why I said those stupid things."

Ten minutes went by as she started to pack for home. Downstairs there was the train schedule so she thought she could look it over and when it was around an hour away from leaving she would call a cab to take her there. Another twenty minutes went by, and her phone rang, it was George! "Hello, my man." This was what she called him in private.

As he listened to her words, he waited and then said "I'm parked outside if you're ready to leave."

"Yes, I'll be right down there, I'm already packed, and ready to go."

On the drive back home to Three Rivers George and Shelia opened up about a lot of things. Early in the journey, Shelia spent most of the time apologizing to George. He didn't seem to need her apology; he was more interested in hearing why she was so protective of her money that he had no interest in. Once she told him all about what Jake did, he understood the hurt, and why she was so protective. To make things easy for her, he suggested that he wanted a prenuptial. This started a long and tedious conversation.

"What do you mean you want to have a prenuptial?"

Answering her very quickly, he said "because that money belongs to your children."

About five minutes went by as she thought; *he wants to free me of a worry concerning my children's inheritance. That would help my fears of what might happen, but if I don't trust him enough to share all that's in my control, what does that say about my trust in him?* Feeling so conflicted about what he said because it was what she had mentioned to her mom before.

She wished that this could all be put behind them and to just move on, but would it be that easy? Would George allow her to share her money with him? Knowing that he did not want one penny because he knew it would only come with many conditions. What was she thinking during this time, and what would she say next?

"No, I don't want that, I was wrong."

"Wrong about what, do you mean you wanted a prenuptial? When were you going to tell me?"

"George, I talked with my mom about that, and we both agreed that wasn't needed."

"Damn it, Shelia, you seem always to do something to try and destroy what we have achieved. Why are you doing this?"

His words were not meant to hurt her, but only to find out what the problem was. Truly he wanted to spend his life with her, but if she could not do away with her adverse past events that just brought on more problems, then he couldn't continue with their plans. As he drove on listening to her sob, he thought; *is this what it will take for her to put this all away? Does she need to realize that trying to control everything will only cause more trouble? I will wait until she stops crying to see what she says next.*

Timing wasn't on his side since they only had about thirty minutes left before arriving at his home. He didn't have time to talk with her, and she would be leaving to go home soon after arriving. What should I do? What should I do? This is what he was thinking; *we have another rough start, I want to get through this, and I think I would feel better if we signed a prenuptial.* A lot of things were put out in the open, but the current prenuptial situation wasn't going to work.

When they arrived, she went straight into the house and headed for the bathroom. Before following after her inside, he put her suitcase in her car, and then went inside. By that time she was finishing up, then right when he opened the front door, she stepped into the hallway and walked toward the door. He stopped by the front door, and asked "are you okay?"

She smiled a little and said "I think so, how about you?"

Knowing she wasn't going to be there that much longer, his words needed to be hopeful, and so he said "Shelia, I will pick you up on Friday."

A little bit surprised and pleasantly hopeful she said "I look forward to that."

"Please call me when you get home tonight."

"Yes, George."

"I love you."

"I love you very much," she said and then walked out the door without a kiss.

CHAPTER 19

They worked the prenuptial out. Shelia talked it over with her mom and her mom gave her an idea on how to fix it. By turning the question around, then presenting a scenario to him about what if another woman that he wanted to marry had something terrible happen to her? Would you go and create a bunch of controls in the hopes of never being hurt like that again. Even if those controls involved not trusting the new girl that you loved so much? He understood and agreed with her stand on a prenuptial which was a giant step for her in trusting him.

It was now his turn to reassure her of his commitment to their future marriage. He requested her to go with him to Three Rivers and he took her to one of the parks and had something to give to her. She was willing to indulge him, so she went along for the ride. It was a little chilly, but still a nice day with gloves on. Parking the car he smiled and said "this is something my mom did for us when we went to town." Taking her by the hand, he walked her to the bridge, and proceeded to take her to the middle. There, he let her know that his commitment was as strong as that bridge. He said "every time you see this bridge I want you to think about how strong my commitment to you is."

What a blessing that these two made it through the first few months of the year and were now getting ready to tie the knot. It wasn't easy; there were times that they both thought it wasn't going to happen, but each time one or both of them would stop, and think about all the good they had in front of them by being together. April in the Midwest can bring on any weather and with only one month left before their wedding the snow came. It came in bunches. They spent the weekend at his home, and the kids had a blast. Peter and his wife were flying in, in three weeks to help them prepare for the wedding.

The weeks went by fast and slow, fast for Shelia because she was trying to arrange everything, and slow for George because he was looking forward to their honeymoon. Somehow he was looking past the wedding, was cold feet, or maybe just thinking about their honeymoon. In his thoughts he treated it as if it had already happened. The truth is that they were both nervous, very nervous.

George was hesitant or maybe just scared? Either way, he had his good friend Calvin there to give him more than just encouragement. According to Calvin, he was there to give George a "swift kick in the ass!"

"Calvin! Calm down! I'm going to get married today. I just have so many memories flooding in from former days."

"I see your point."

Even though it was on his mind he avoided telling the story of his former wife, because it was a very heartbreaking one, and today was going to be a happy one.

They were there in the room, all dressed in their tuxes and ready to shine. George had one thought going through his mind; *I wonder how beautiful Shelia will look in her wedding dress? I Guess I'll have to wait and see for myself.* He then smiled with a big grin, big enough for Calvin to ask. "What's so funny big guy?"

"Oh, nothing really, I was thinking about how beautiful Shelia must be in her dress. Then I thought about it, and it occurred to me that I would have to leave this room, walk down the aisle, and marry her to find out." He then made a very sly gesture with his hands. Calvin wasn't even sure what it meant and he thought it was better not to ask.

She had been married before, so her thoughts were that it was no big deal. *No big deal, no big deal... NO BIG DEAL!* Her friends were there for encouragement, like Tammy (Calvin's wife) who was there to offer her support, and a laugh or two which Shelia really didn't appreciate. Some said that she should wear her mother's dress, but quickly she shot that one down saying "I've done that before and I have no desire to do it again.

"Breathe, breathe" was all her daughter could say right now, while looking at her mom trying to fit into that dress, that seemed to cause her pain.

Shelia stopped wiggling, turned around, and said to her "thank you dear, but mom's having a time getting this princess outfit on."

Putting on the makeup first before the dress was a good idea and at the same time it was a bad idea. It saved some time, but with all that movement to put on the dress caused a little smear to appear on her left shoulder strap. Luckily it was the end of the strap and was easily tucked away inside the dress. Her headpiece was now being attached, and then she put on the shoes. *No hurry, there was plenty of time* Shelia thought until some lady opened the door and said "ten minutes."

George was ready, very ready, to do this. His thoughts were now on how much he'd wished he had been married before, but when his first love ended so tragically, he accepted that it was his only chance. Taking a deep breath, he said to himself *I'm going to make the best of this opportunity and be the best man I can be for her.*

Calvin took George by the arm and said "Come on buddy let's move out and take our places in your wedding, I'm sure you want to be ready when Shelia walks down the aisle."

"I want to be there for her in all parts of her life from this day forward."

Calvin stopped and paused for a second and then said "that my friend is a wonderful plan. Let's hope that we will always be there for our girls."

George and his best man stood there ready to receive Shelia as she was walked down the aisle by her son Steven. George remembered her fear of him wanting her for her family's money, he smiled because he couldn't help but find that funny.

Now that the sweat had been wiped from her forehead, they were ready to bring her out. She was feeling very light headed because she didn't think she would ever be married again. Her friends took her by the hand and carefully walked her down the hall with a young teenager holding her dress up in the back. Step by step until she reached those double doors to the sanctuary and there she stopped breathing!

Her friends passed her off to her son, who noticed that she wasn't breathing, and said "mom what are you doing? Are you holding your breath?"

Letting out all the pent-up air and then gasping large amounts back in, she answered "yes, Steven, I'm so scared."

Bridges of Three Rivers

Before he started to walk, even though the music had just begun he turned to her, and said "George is a good man mom, he loves us more than anything."

With that said, they both turned and started their ascent towards the minister. Rose petals covered her path, the yard was green, and spring was in the air. There was the smell of the lake blended with the flowers that were set all around. George spared no expense to make his home so beautiful for this wonderful day. Her thoughts were only on how moving in and spending the rest of her days with him would be so beautiful.

Then slowly they had stopped in front of the minister, who said "who gives this bride away?"

In which her son said "I do." Then he gave her hand to the minister and then went to stand beside the best man.

What a picture these two were, both successful people who had lived many years, and done many things. Now they were ready to share all they had with one another, for better or for worse, for richer or for poorer, till death do they part. I guess that says it all. Now the minister said the most important words "you may kiss the bride."

Their reception was awesome and the kids ran around the yard and played by the lake. The grown-ups went inside for drinks and dancing. He remembered their first dance way back in Chicago and after the speeches were made, the cake was cut, and the wine poured. It was now time to dance, the song they both agreed on was then played, and he took her hand.

On the dance floor they were all alone, the lights dimmed, and everyone watched as they danced. They had been learning the foxtrot just for that night. He whisked her around, padded her right shoulder then they took off. Sidestepping, spinning, sidestepping and then facing each other for some more steps, and another spin or two. The crowd was all in amazement, enjoying their moves. She didn't want the music to end, to her this was the most important night ever, and for that night she truly felt like a queen.

As soon as the song ended several men were asking for the next dance with Shelia. She was just so lovely that night and George felt her radiance on the dance floor. Being the gentleman that he was he gladly relinquished her hand to the first person who wanted a dance with her. There was this woman who thought she was wonderful too and wanted to dance with her.

He took a seat and gathered his thoughts and he reasoned that; *why not share her tonight, for tomorrow she will be mine, all mine in this lifetime.* Since he didn't have any children, he was happy to love, and care for hers. There was the talk of adopting them, but they thought it was not a good idea to remove the family name they already had. I mean it wouldn't be right to judge an entire clan for the mistakes of one person.

Calvin noticed him sitting there all alone while poor Shelia couldn't leave the dance floor.

"Sit down" George said, "I'm not going anywhere."

"What about your carriage, won't it turn into a pumpkin at midnight?" Calvin said to him while patting him on the back.

"Funny, I guess she's Cinderella then?"

"Enough of that, where are you two going for your honeymoon?"

"Calvin, you know where we're going, I've been talking with you about that for weeks. We're going to the French Riviera for three weeks!"

"Oh yeah, that's right, rub it in, why don't you?"

"Sorry buddy, we'll bring you back some red Bordeaux. Look, look, I think she's done dancing. She just waved off that man she had danced with before. I suppose she's made all the rounds?"

As she walked towards George, Shelia was worn out. George noticed that, and he quickly stood up and put his arms around her, then said "my dear you are surely the life of the party."

"Thank you, my sweet man, but my name is not Shirley."

"Hah, you are so funny, but I love you anyway."

She looked around and noticed that it was getting late then she asked George "when are we leaving?"

"We can leave tonight the plane is ready to go."

"Let's go before we get too tired."

With that said they stood up, waved at their family and friends, then turned, and headed for the door.

Calvin looked at his wife and said "there they go, off to see beautiful places."

Their wedding was different, eye-opening, the children were precious, and now that it was over the honeymoon was even better! Where are they, isn't that the question? After a night of intense intimacy they were plain tired out, worn out was a more appropriate term. They had breakfast in bed at 10:30 am which was early for them that day, but there was a schedule of things to do. They walked to the sliding glass door, pulled open the curtains, then opened the door, and sat down on the patio with their breakfast tray. They looked out at the water, smelling the air, and enjoying this wonderful first day together as Mr. and Mrs. Esperanza.

These two weeks will be spent traveling the area, eating some fine French cuisine, and enjoying time on a sailboat on the Mediterranean. It will be time spent with each other where there won't be a care in the world, or anybody to give them grief. She had come up with one damn good honeymoon. These will be days of love for each other, enjoying the wine, the dancing, meeting the indigenous people, and certainly blending into one fantastic person. They are equally strong, kind, gracious, and of course, both medical doctors. These two weeks together that they would always look back on and do again.

CHAPTER 20

"All the checks have been made, now let's call in our destination to the tower and then fly off." They were not ready to fly overseas yet, but they wanted to go to the coast, and spend a day before heading across the ocean. Since his brother had volunteered to watch the place for a week, he didn't need to take him home to North Carolina. Therefore tonight they were headed for Cape Hatteras, North Carolina.

The honeymoon was on George's mind for months, whereas believed that the plan had started in his soul before he was even aware of it. He used to read about the French Riviera when he was in the Air Force and his thoughts were; *what a wonderful place to be for at least a couple of weeks.* Before making these plans, he did a lot of research. Shelia had traveled through so much pain and hurt. This honeymoon was to be an opportunity for her to reset her life and put it on a path of blessings.

Bridges of Three Rivers

George woke up early as soon as daybreak had set in although they had arrived at the beach house around 2 am. When the sun rose over the Atlantic he wanted to see it, Shelia was content to sleep, but he wasn't going to let her miss that beautiful moment. Besides, his opinion was that she could return to bed after witnessing that spectacle with him.

"This is magnificent, worth waking up even after only a few hours of sleep," she said to him as they looked to the east over the beautiful ocean.

With his arm around her, he squeezed her tight and said: "yes it is dear and I planned for many weeks to experience this with you today."

Several moments went by until he noticed the silence break with a tiny little snooze from his lovely bride. With her head on his shoulder it wasn't easy to move her without disturbing her sleep. At least that's what he thought until he stood up and then quickly lifted her up and carried her to bed. After a gentle kiss on her forehead or her third eye, he then returned to the deck.

As Shelia slept, he sat there on the deck, drinking some scotch, and smoking a cigar while watching the waves come in and out. He reflected on how they had met in Chicago, only to find out that they lived relatively close to each other. Then he remembered how through several misunderstandings their chance of becoming lovers was almost ruined. He wondered if this was meant to be, or if he had missed some important signs, or was he just over thinking about it? One thing he knew at this moment was that he couldn't remember a time when he felt this happy and at peace. The scotch and cigar certainly helped calm his mind.

After a jog along the beach, then a shower, he was ready for breakfast. Shelia was still asleep, so he devised a plan to wake her up. He looked around the kitchen, found the needed tools, and the provisions to carry out that plan. With the grits in the pot boiling, the eggs frying, and the bread toasting, he poured the orange juice. He put the breakfast on the plates and placed them on the table board then went up to the room. Lying on the bed, and barely asleep, Shelia heard him walk in.

George gently kissed her on the back of the neck and said "my queen your breakfast is served."

They spent the rest of the day enjoying each other in many ways. It was as if they had deprived themselves of this joy for too many years. Anyway, their day spent on the beaches of North Carolina would be remembered. In the morning they would board their charter jet and fly across the Atlantic on their way to Spain and then the French Riviera.

The first stop was in Madrid then on to the French Riviera. Their chartered plane was capable of traveling up to 500 miles an hour and at an altitude of

41,000 feet. George had spent all his savings on this three-week honeymoon, and he was very confident that it would be more than worth every penny. Besides, he chuckled later when he found out how rich Shelia was. Shelia said nothing about the expenses; she liked all the special amenities that money could buy, especially since she had refused its appeal all those years.

The three days they stayed in Madrid were awesome where they went to the coast and enjoyed the local cuisine. Being a big tennis fan, George took her to see the professional tennis center, where a tournament was being played leading up to the French Open. He had a plan to travel there for one day to watch the French Open. He went with her to do some shopping for clothes and also she had a few items she wanted to purchase for some friends back home.

On the train to France, they were mesmerized by how beautiful the coastline was. This little French town that they were going to spend three weeks in was very quiet, and therefore it was an appealing town. They went up the stairs and into their room, there they threw the bags on the bed, and went to the balcony to peer out over the ocean. After several minutes of looking out on the ocean, their noses started to detect the fine French cuisine from a restaurant down the street.

She looked at him and said "George, I want some of that food and wine so let's get out of here."

He picked up his wallet and then told her "let's go downstairs and see if we need reservations. Then we can walk there."

"Sounds like a nice plan, my man."

The desk clerk told them that the restaurants in that town weren't that busy. They thanked him then walked out the front door to get some food. Just walking and holding hands, what a sweet site. Many people noticed them and said hello or winked at them. Upon entering the restaurant, the hostess greeted them in French, which both could speak pretty well. Once seated their menus were handed to them, and after ordering, the head waitress showed up with the wine list. With an opportunity to taste several brands, they finally settled on one.

It was a great evening of food, wine, and dancing. On the next day they were traveling to Paris to visit the Louvre museum. Then to the Eiffel Tower to see the night lights of Paris. Lunch on this corner cafe' was so picturesque that Shelia had their waiter take several pictures. They spent most of their lunchtime talking about how wonderful things would be for their new family. Breathing the night air and looking out over that city of love he put his arm around her neck then drew her closer for a very sensual kiss; a kiss that he had wanted to give her ever since they made it up to the top.

Bridges of Three Rivers

On day three in France, they had no schedule, just things they wanted to see, and they had twenty-one days to do it. For them, this honeymoon would be a great chance to find a deeper understanding of each other. George was certainly a thinker so when he thought about life and relationships he made sure their time spent together being undisturbed was paramount. And with this thing called "jet lag" behind them, they were now starting to get on the local time zone.

He used the washroom, headed downstairs, and made breakfast. The early breakfast only consisted of fruit, hot tea, and then an English muffin. Once he had accomplished all that he set out to wake her up. Putting the knife down after slicing the fruit he began to turn around and make his walk upstairs. Then to his surprise, while making his turn, he noticed a shadow and then heard "good morning, my handsome man. I see you made breakfast for us."

Catching his breath he smiled, then said "it's a good thing I put that knife down. You scared the hell out of me. Please, in the future don't sneak up on me like that. You know I've had extensive military training."

"Okay George, I see we have a lot to learn about each other."

After saying that, they both went out to the patio to enjoy their breakfast, and the beautiful morning on the French Riviera.

"I don't know what this cost you, but I love it," he said with his hands in the air admiring the beautiful

Mediterranean Sea from this French Riviera city of Nice, France.

Standing behind him, she put her arms around his waist, and said "anything for you my main and only man."

They waited for an hour, and then they decided it was time to go for a walk along the shore. Something that both had dreamed of doing was now happening. They walked while holding hands, even an occasional swing of the arms, this incredible feeling of love just had to be felt, and not explained. Approaching a long pier, they looked at each other and agreed to walk down to the end. What happened when they reached the end wasn't planned or even talked about. It was as spontaneous as it could be.

With the smell of the ocean, the feel of the sun on their back, and the sites of that gorgeous place, they realized that their hands had turned to look out, then after taking in a few deep breaths, they turned around towards each other. Their hands reached out to hold each other and that was what their souls so much desired at that moment. Their heads slightly turned and targeting the lips in front of them. This kiss, ah this kiss, it wasn't sloppy like you see in the movies. No, this kiss was near perfection. Slow, smooth, gentle, and with a form of passion that seemed to radiate out.

After finishing satisfying one of their desires of the moment they heard clapping. *Clapping!* George thought *I wonder what's going on that we have missed.*

Both looked around to find nothing else happening except for the people on the dock looking at them and smiling. This brought a smile to his face, but Shelia's face turned red. He laughed and said to her "my dear, you are simply amazing, and all these people here are a testimony to that."

"Thanks, my sweet man. I'm sure a handsome man like you didn't hurt the applause, especially from the ladies."

Soaking in this moment they stayed a little longer than planned. Talking with the locals and gaining more critical information. Like the location of the best wineries, restaurants, and hiking trails. He put his arm around her waist and turned her around 180 degrees. It was then that they followed this vector to leave the pier. With the passing of time they were both getting hungry. Also, after talking with the locals, they discovered that one of the restaurants was within walking distance of the beach.

Their table was full of roses and they were so beautiful that George had wondered *maybe one of the locals heard us mention coming here and called this in?* Either way, it was a classy thing to do.

Shelia sat there and contemplated how wonderful this man she married was. Her thoughts were; *I wonder if I will be good enough for him, damn what am I now thinking? I can't go questioning if I'm good enough, of course, I am! I have to believe I am, or*

else I will always doubt myself, and that will never work.
Time seemed to go incredibly slow while her thoughts
were on this.

"A penny for your thoughts" he said, noticing
the look in her eyes that she was far away.

"My dear George, my thoughts are so mixed up
right now that I don't think it would be right to share
them with you."

This was something that he decided to leave
alone and let her choose when to share with him. The
waitress had a big smile for them while she asked for
their order. Shelia found it better to enjoy her time with
George, so she then engaged in some girl talk with the
waitress who just seemed eager to oblige. Meeting the
people there that day caused them to fall into the trap
of wishing they could live there. Both agreed that they
would return often.

A week had gone by and as much as they had
loved their visit to France, and especially Paris, they
were now ready to rest for at least a couple of days.
That night Shelia decided to cook dinner, and to her
surprise, she learned that George was quite the chef
too. Not only could he cook breakfast, but making
dinner was his specialty. Laughing at her surprise on
how well he could handle himself in the kitchen, but
tonight he just wanted to be her sous-chef.

Lighting the candles, he turned to her, and said
"you look beautiful tonight and my chef prepared a

magnificent dinner for us."

"I bet this chef is amazing!" She said as she gracefully walked down the stairs.

With a cough, George said "I heard that her sous-chef was amazing too!"

With the candles lit, the lights dimmed very low, and the wine poured. Now everything was perfect; they had their first dinner meal in France alone over light casual conversations mostly about the sites that they had seen so far. There wasn't an agenda for either one of them, time together alone was certainly on the list, but what happened next was a surprise...!

"Dinner was so good tonight, I believe you, and I should open up our own restaurant" George said toasting a final glass of wine.

"That could work, that could work" She said that with such conviction!

After putting the dishes away and cleaning the table these two newlyweds went into the den to relax. Relaxing? I guess maybe dancing was their way of doing that. George turned on some slow jazz and turned the lights up just a little bit, then stepping so casually and so romantically, he strolled over to her. Bending over he extended out his hand towards her and said "my lovely lady, may I have this dance?"

She said no words; instead, she looked into his eyes and stood up. Following him to the middle of the floor and then putting her arms over his shoulders. With his hands on her waist, everything felt like a perfect fit.

Slowly moving, no particular steps, just two people in love holding each other close. He could smell the warmth of her neck. Noticing her perfume had blended with her scent to create a sweet smell that only excited his senses. Her chin resting on his shoulder, she couldn't help but notice how strong his shoulders were. Then music ended too soon, way too soon. So, they just stayed that way, and danced for three more tunes.

Once they had agreed to take a break. It didn't take them long to realize that dancing was over for the night. He took her hand after some passionate kisses and then they went to their bedroom. After some time in bed then the whirlpool, they decided to go downstairs for a snack. While in the kitchen Shelia made some coffee because that night she wasn't too eager to sleep.

The sun was up! In fact it had been up for a few hours! George then sprang up out of bed, pulled back a part of the shades to notice the spectacle of waking up so late. Looking at his gorgeous bride still sleeping, *so beautiful, she's so cute. God, please be with me every day, fill me with your love, and help me, help me to give her my love every day.* He turned around then gently walked out of the room.

Smiling as he put on his apron, he thought of how much pleasure cooking with her the previous night brought. Reaching into the fridge, he pulled out eggs and after finding some fresh vegetables, he thought of what else was needed. *Hum, let's see, eggs, vegetables, cream, what else can I use? Ah, Gouda cheese. That will complete the frittata; I will make it the way my mom taught me.* He brewed some special herbal tea then warmed up some scones that they had purchased the day before. The kitchen started to take on a very strong aromatic scent. Then the bedroom door crept open.

"It smells so good down here that I couldn't sleep any longer. You know that your great cooking caused me to cut my sleep short?"

George put his thumbs under his apron then with a big grin said "all in my plans dear, all in my plans."

"I wonder what other plans you have for me. Oh, wait I think we probably did some of them last night. What wonderful plans you do have?"

After eating this awesome meal, then enjoying the scones with their tea, they were fulfilled spiritually and physically. She seemed to be a little lethargic and he didn't question why. Instead he just stood up and kissed her on the forehead then cleared the table. As he returned from the kitchen he stopped in his tracks to notice her.

CHAPTER 21

Crying, crying, but why? And as he approached, she seemed to cry even harder. At first, he thought that he was causing her pain, but couldn't understand why? He sat down next to her and asked "what's wrong sweetheart?"

Shelia tried to think of what to tell him, but she just couldn't find the words to say. Instead, she only said "I can't say. I can't find the reason why I'm crying."

"Dear we have nothing to do today, so let's spend it going deep into all of our past problems, and disappointments. I'll start "my dad died when I was young. He was in Vietnam fighting for what he thought was right."

"I heard something about that from your brother. How do you think that affected you?"

He went on to share with her the disappointments in his young life of the things he could have learned from his dad. He was never angry at his father; in fact, he treated his memory like he was a hero. Listening to him speak of all the things he thought he missed and because of that she started to compare it with the fact that her daddy was there for her. Somehow she couldn't square it with his definition of a dad being heroic certainly not hers.

Shelia was now crying and for a good reason; George's stories of losing his dad and then George telling her how strong his mom was through all that. Through her tears, she was able to ask him more detailed questions as to how his mom managed to raise two boys on the farm. As wonderful as she was, she however did have support from her in-laws, who owned a farm and moved her and the boys there. So, they talked about that part of his life at length, and then that hurt was resolved.

"Wow, that was interestingly productive in solving one of the deep voids in my soul," he said.

She sat there looking so hard at him that he thought she was glaring! He broke the silence and said "why are you staring at me?"

"George, I'm sorry, I didn't mean to do that. I was thinking real hard about my problems with my dad growing up. I don't want to compare our dads, there's no way to do that properly, and who knows how things might have turned out had your dad lived. I am not insinuating that he might not have been a great one, just that he was in a war, and that is a tragic situation to deal with. I'm trying to say what I feel without hurting any memory or projection you might have had about him. If I did, I'm sorry."

He wanted to respond to her that he wasn't in the least bit angry. He was very impressed with her deep thoughts on this matter. A mystery to him was that he couldn't come up with any words to say and the silence just made her feel worse. *Now I did it! I made her cry because I can't respond to her. I better tell her that I'm fine with what she said.*

Forming these words he quickly said "dear, I am so proud of your deep understanding of the fatalities of this life and especially the one involving my dad in the war. Please stop crying, please stop or you'll make me start, and you don't want that, do you?"

This made her smile, and then when she saw how goofy he looked, she started to laugh. Since she was laughing and they had put to bed the story or the image of his dad, he asked her. "Okay now that we are finished with putting my dad's dead memory to bed. What about your past with your dad? Are you over whatever problems you might have had with him?"

She was taken aback, but not in a bad way. Instead she was ready to talk about that. What surprised her was that she didn't think he wanted to know. Then remembering how cold her first husband was, she said "thank you for asking, I believe it would do me some good to put all of that past on the table. Maybe we can chop it up, bread it, fry it, and then feed it to a big monster."

Bridges of Three Rivers

"Well then, what was the biggest problem you had with your dad?"

She giggled and then answered "the fact that I wasn't born a boy."

There was no response from him, but he only nodded his head, followed by an inquisitive look. Then she went on to detail how he would always try to get her to join the softball team. How he wanted her to follow him into business. For many years she felt like a big disappointment because those things didn't seem to please her, but she wanted to please her daddy. Her mom wasn't really of big help because she seemed to be caught up in the life of a wealthy woman. Shelia explained to George that she didn't mean to judge her mom, in fact, she loved her dearly.

After she had finished explaining her problems, he said "wow that was a good download unload. Do you feel any better? If not, let's try to break all of that down and then put it to rest."

"When did you become a shrink?"

"Ha!" He said. Then after taking a breath he went on to explain how his mom would take him to the bridges of Three Rivers and use them as focal points to explain the secrets of life.

Amazed about this, Shelia went on to quiz him on what all that meant. Then after a brief explanation, he said "now let's discuss your not being born a boy."

"It was a trial for me in my early years to try and please him. It seemed that everything I did in life had to center around learning to take over the business."

George then interjected, "when did this start?"

"Oh who knows for sure, I'm sure in his mind it was as soon as he learned that my mom could have no more children."

To explore this subject more, she explained how marrying the salesman that her dad had approved of was a disaster. He learned how her first husband who gave her two wonderful children tried to sidestep her to obtain the rights to her inheritance. George started to understand how this would be a deep problem for her and especially in trusting men again. She even went on to tell him about how she tried a life of romance with women. Never marrying again, but coming close to doing so in Seattle.

"Well, how do you feel now?"

Putting her arm around his shoulder, she said "much better; it feels so good to unload this. We need to put all these past troubles behind us and move on with our new lives together."

A funny thing happened through all this pain, they both felt very contented and happy to have each other. They noticed it was now dark and they were very hungry. So after some discussion, they decided to go into the kitchen and prepare a splendid meal together.

They spent the next few days with an unbelievable height of conscious awareness. It seems that wherever they went people just wanted their company. George talked with Shelia about how the people they would meet seemed to gravitate to them. They didn't look like tourists and they spoke French very well.

So what was different? Shelia came up with one very plausible answer and when he heard it he resonated with her conclusion. After that, she said "ever since we talked a few days ago about digging deep into our souls and releasing all the negative memories, we are more in tune with the beauty of this current existence."

He replied "wow, I believe you've hit the nail on the head. Not that I believe life is full of nails and that we are the hammer, but that you correctly defined what is happening to us."

"Well George, I believe because I am aware that we should live our lives in a strong faith in God."

They were both raised as Catholics. Therefore, the beliefs that they were taught were very common. With that, they both had a common path to work from. He had always stayed in the church mostly to please his mother, but had some questions on how the leaders believed what they did. Shelia stopped going to church shortly after her divorce, and with her experimenting with the gay lifestyle, she wasn't sure how the church would perceive her?

They now felt very confident and in tune, very peaceful, and very comfortable in their life. That night was to be the beginning of their track into religion and what it meant to them. George belonged to a lodge, and he learned more lessons there that helped him become a better man. Most importantly to him was that he learned from the military and the lodge how to be calm in the face of controversy. Religion wasn't something he protected, but when she started talking, she put him a little bit on the defensive.

"Okay you believe in the church, do you also believe in all the tragic things the church does, and did in the name of God?"

"I see where this is going, you want to point out all the negative things about the church, and I presume we are only talking about the Christian church?"

"Sure, that is as good a place to start as any."

"Right, there were many bad things that the church did in the name of God, and we were warned about this by the disciple John. When he said, and I paraphrase that, *they will kill you and think they are doing God's service.* So that's nothing to hang your hat on, many people have killed others for their own misguided reasons."

"Okay, what about when these church people say we must go to church. They go as far as to say that is where you will find God. Does this mean to limit where the creator of the universe can be?"

George now understood that she had done her homework and in answering her, he wanted to use the Holy Bible to provide the answers. He said "another great question, Paul talked about a time coming when people would claim to believe in God, but deny that God had any power."

It was almost like she had rehearsed these questions, but on realizing that he wasn't answering like other people do caused her to skip to a more undefinable question, or at least one that she thought was. Walking into the kitchen, she turned around and asked him if he wanted some coffee.

She returned with two cups of a good French roast and then said "who is God? Is God a person, a man, or simply God is Jesus?"

Understanding the direction she was going helped him to formulate the final nail in this coffin of who God is. So he went back to the Bible and said "many people know not who God is and this causes problems. They assume that they are not meant to know or that this identity can't be known. Yes, some people want to believe that Jesus is God and although this is partially correct, it is not something to peg all the laws on."

Not that he did this on purpose to confuse her, but he didn't give her the answer because he wanted first to eliminate the false or partial ones. Waiting for her to say something he took a couple of sips of coffee.

"Are you going to tell me who or what God is?"

"Yes I will, but the first thing that we need to learn is in the New Testament and that is; God is not a man and therefore he cannot lie. In other words, man lies so God cannot be a man. These words are in the books written by John and many of the teachings that Jesus did confirm who God is. God is simply Love, when we love one another then in that instant we are in God."

Shelia sat and listened intently, but still had questions, many questions indeed.

CHAPTER 22

Once the first week was over, and knowing that it was full of positive interactions, these newlyweds were now ready to enjoy the beauty of France. They had visited most of the sites and met a lot of friendly people, and of course, they went deep into their new-found knowledge of each other.

Their rental was someone's home that was vacant while they went on a long sabbatical or something. George didn't feel the need to ask, he just wanted to rent a home, where he intended to spend the last week or two just living together. *A honeymoon should not last more than ten days* he thought. Time spent just living and not vacationing was a good way to see how life together might be.

Working together in the kitchen went very well, especially since both were good cooks. He was old school in some ways, but being raised by his mother did help him to appreciate women much more than other men would. During his time growing up, he would do the laundry, and not expect his mom to do it. One day Shelia asked him if he would take out the trash when he was done chopping some onions. He looked at her sitting on the couch and said "why? Are your legs broken?"

His mom would take the garbage out, mow the lawn, and work on the farm until the boys were big enough to pitch in. Living on the farm allowed her to be home when he and his brother were finished with school. His mom was a great teacher to the boys for she knew how to make the best of things. Though she wasn't a Buddhist monk or anything like that she seemed to have a lot of that deeper knowledge. Being a Christian, she would read and study the Bible, learning from one of this world's greatest masters.

They walked along the coastline holding hands and kissing every morning. Is it possible that they could keep up this high level of love? Maybe, just maybe, these two people had stamina that came from many years of doing what was good in the world. Shelia was missing her children that day. Though she didn't want to let him know that, but since she was very quiet, he suspected something was wrong.

"What's wrong my dear?"

"Oh, it's nothing."

George wasn't ready to push her to open up then. On that matter his thoughts were; *really nothing huh? I bet she is probably missing her children, but we still have another week.* He paused and then thought; *I know what to say that might help her.* He then suggested "maybe we can call them tonight and do some FaceTime?"

Wiping the tears away, she said "can we?"

"Of course we can, why can't we?"

"I don't know, I thought that maybe you didn't want any distractions during our honeymoon?"

Her statement brought on some concern, and he thought *does she think that way of me? I mean does she think I'm that overbearing not to feel she is free to do whatever she wants to do?* Just the thought of her thinking this way about him brought on some tears. She noticed this and said "why are you crying? Did I say something that hurt you?"

"No, it wasn't so much that you said anything to hurt me. I just don't want to be perceived as being overbearing to anyone. I've never been pushy or strict, but then again I've never raised children."

Knowing that he needed an explanation, she said "I'm so sorry I think I was putting on you all the things that I've experienced from the men in my life. I happen to know that you aren't that way, you are a very kind free-willing soul."

"Thanks, I needed that. Now let's remember that we are not a fifty-fifty partnership. We should take on 100 percent each that way nothing falls through the cracks."

"Good point, now let's make that call" she said.

Some time on the phone with her children made a big difference.

On their walk along the shoreline that morning Shelia asked George some questions. He wasn't sure if answering them would be beneficial, but a perfect day was starting so he felt the spirit of the Sun reaching into his soul. Holding her hand, smelling the morning ocean, and listening to the birds sing. He couldn't help but think *I wish this day would never end because I am so much in love with her.* Probably he shouldn't have sat on these thoughts.

She squeezed his hand and said "tell me about your first love. I know it had a tragic ending, but I'm curious."

This question was something he didn't expect. Breathing deeply, he thought about what or how much he would say. For some reason, he acted like it could be a question to trick him, but quickly realized that it couldn't be. Then he proceeded to tell her all about how much he loved her and how they planned on spending their lives together. She already knew about the car accident and the baby, so he didn't mention that for a second time to her.

She got a perspective from this story of his first love and the fact that until then he hadn't given his heart to another person. Finally, she felt the last part of her heart had been cleansed of fear. Now with this man in her life she could be free to love again and to give all of her heart to another. What happened that night was something she had never experienced.

She fell asleep, a deep sleep, for that day was full of activity. She left her body and into a dream, a very disturbing dream. In that dream she was on the top of a skyscraper, leaning over like she was going to fall, and that looking down caused her to become fearful. Not falling or jumping off, she just looked down, and that made her very afraid.

Not that she snored or made noise, but she woke up to notice that she wasn't breathing. All she could think was; *am I dying? I can think, but I can't breathe, I need to breathe.* She had a fright that she had never experienced before and taking ten deep controlled breaths helped her fall back to sleep, but only to wake up again. *What is going on, I'm so cold. Maybe this is it, maybe I'm not going to wake up? There I go again not breathing. I'll do ten deep breaths again.*

This ended in the morning, but not late, in fact, it was early. Surprised that she woke up, all she could do was lay there, and wonder why she didn't die last night before he woke up. There lying next to her man, she realized that she was going to live, and that her life needed to mean more than it had. *But what happened last night?* That was the only thing she could think about. She felt compelled to wake him up.

"George. Honey, are you going to wake up?"

"What time is it?"

"Uh, it's 4:32," she said very sheepishly.

"OMG it's 4:30! What's wrong?"

"I had a bad dream about dying and woke up a few times holding my breath. I wasn't sure if I was dying or having an asthma attack, but I don't have asthma."

"What did you do to get through it?"

"I took deep breathes until I went back to sleep, but I was worried I wouldn't wake up each time."

Remembering the things his mom would teach him on those bridges of Three Rivers. He told her something his mom had told him when he was just a little boy. It happened after his dad died in the war. George didn't know why he had to die and his mom wanted to tell him the whole story, but she felt at his age he wouldn't understand.

"When I was young my mom explained to me why people had to die. I was very young, so she put it this way "son your daddy went to Vietnam because our country needed him to join some other Americans to defend those people over there. I asked her why we had to send people over there to Vietnam. Then she told me that Jesus said that to sacrifice oneself to protect others is a great thing to do."

"George that's all well and good your dad was a hero. Now, what does that have to do with my dreams?"

"Oh yeah, that's true. She went on to explain that in this life you must be willing to die every day to be grateful. I didn't know what she meant until she said we can't live in fear of death or else happiness in life does not exist."

Explaining this to her in pieces seemed to work to where she said "now I get it, I had a dark night of the soul last night, right?"

"I do believe that's what you had. The important thing is not to fear death."

"Okay now, where's my breakfast?"

"It's just waiting for us dear to cook."

They proceeded into the kitchen where the conversation continued. Shelia wanted to understand how she could get to the point where death was not a concern in her life. According to her, everyone feared death, and that was only natural. Listening to him explain to her how wise his mom was impressed her even more. He was beating the eggs, and she asked "do you think you can teach me how not to fear death?"

"I would love to do nothing more. The best time to start is right now. The first thing you need to learn is that we are all connected, in doing that you will see people, and things in a different light."

She then asked "how so?"

"When you treat others as you would like to be treated you will find that the love in the universe flows out to you. Even if you notice a bad situation, you can find the wisdom to not engage in whatever bad energy is going on. Instead, you will learn how to quickly assess it, and say kind words to either bring calm to the problem or find a way to escape it."

"Those are very wise words. Did your mom teach them to you after you were in a fight?"

"Good guess, I needed a lot of guidance early on in my life."

Their day began with breakfast and some very stimulating conversation. George helped her break down some walls that she had constructed throughout her lifetime. That day they would spend their time together walking along the beach and later have lunch at one of the local spots that they liked. They spent time in town buying some gifts and later went for dinner at their favorite Italian restaurant. The following day they were going to watch a fourth-round tournament of the French Open tennis slam.

CHAPTER 23

Playing tennis was something he liked to do ever since he first watched Andre Agassi win back in 1999. While visiting his brother in North Carolina and also playing when he was stationed at Pope Air Force base near Fayetteville, NC. The clay was so much fun to play on, and George loved the ability to slide to reach some shots. He grew up watching all the great Americans like Michael Chang, Jim Courier, and of course Andre.

He got up early and headed downstairs to prepare breakfast. With the coffee brewing and those eggs simmering breakfast was now ready. *Now to head upstairs and wake her up, we don't have a lot of time to catch the train.* Opening the door, he found her still in bed, and he said "dear we have a date with destiny today."

"What are you talking about, destiny?"

"Well Nadal is in the quarterfinals, and maybe we'll get to see him. If not we could watch Roger Federer."

All went well that morning as George got Shelia downstairs to eat and then taking off down the street to the train station. Getting on the train, she squeezed his hand, and then he kissed her. She knew that he was so excited that day because he had talked about this on the flight from America. The ride was only about an hour, and the sites were magnificent as they traveled along the coast.

Upon arriving there, he dug out his map, and noticed that the walk wasn't very far. They passed a few city blocks, and then they noticed the crowds were walking mainly in one direction toward the stadium. The air that day was very cool, and there was still a little hint of the dew that came in overnight. *It's just a beautiful day to enjoy one of tennis' greatest slams and to watch one of its greatest players.* With a smile on his face, he then thought *yep, either Nadal or Federer, both are great.*

George said "do you want to get a drink before we sit down?"

"That's a great idea" she said.

"We won't be able to get back up until they have a break."

"Who are we watching?"

"I don't know yet; there doesn't seem to be a listing."

"Oh well, get me some mineral water then, maybe a Perrier."

With mineral water bottles in their hands and some snacks, they both made their way to their seats. They made sure to bring hats just in case the sun came out, but now it was hiding behind some clouds. They were finally seated and noticed the scoreboard displaying; Nadal verses Del Porto. "This will be an excellent match!" He said to her.

Back and forth, these two sluggers didn't seem to want to leave the baseline. Just a lot of heavy hitting and neither wanted to bring the other to the net until in the eleventh round of the first set. Nadal had a triple break point, and Juan was starting to show some fatigue. As Rafael returned a very good serve, Juan made his approach to the net for a successful putaway. Not to be deterred, Rafael set a short return of Juan's next serve. Quickly, Juan stepped forward right after his serve, and was ready to make an excellent passing shot.

Now with this pivotal game at deuce, Juan seemed to regain his composure. He delivered a decent second serve that Rafael hit with such determination that he was going to force this point, but instead, Juan took a lot off the speed of this return, and then dropped it about two feet inside the net. Rafael managed to get to it and keep it in play, but only to have Juan return it over his head so he couldn't make a play on that shot. Juan ended up winning his serve, but they went to deuce one more time.

The crowd was so loud in this match and the players gave them plenty to cheer for. Not sure if Nadal was going to win, Juan was giving him all he could handle, and more. Nadal had a very powerful game, but with Juan's height, that made it more difficult for Nadal to hammer out those easy points. Also, Juan had his power and with the first set headed for a tiebreaker should have favored him.

It was six to six, there was a commercial break, and then the start of the tiebreaker would follow. Nadal won his serve, and it was now Juan's turn. He took a quick hit to the inside line and then followed the serve-in. Stunned by this Nadal made a quick adjustment and hit the ball high trying to put it out of Juan's reach. The ball landed just outside of the baseline and it was close enough for Nadal to want a recall. Juan won the point but the next one he didn't. With a great serve and volley, Nadal was ready for it! He batted the ball hard, fast, and with a wicked spin to the outside, right past Juan's backhand.

Juan Del Porto won the first set tiebreaker 12-10. The crowd became very quiet when Nadal started the second set, for it seemed as though they observed that he was getting tired. Watching them play and seeing that Juan would hold his serve under intense distress from Nadal. To George this match seemed to be going Nadal's way. Seeing Shelia was involved in the action he asked her during one of the breaks "do you think Nadal is making a comeback?"

Bridges of Three Rivers

Putting her cup down and then making a face like she was confused, she said "I don't know what to think, to me he appears to be challenging Juan for his serve with a strong determination that I don't know if he can keep it up.

He was going to answer, but they went back out on the court. The score was 3-2 for Nadal and Juan was ready to serve. As he watched this sixth game, it dawned on him that something was happening. *Why isn't Juan chasing down the ball like he did before?* Losing his serve, Juan seemed to be tired, and Nadal went on to win the second set 6-3. It was time to stretch their legs, then to get some more water, and a bathroom break.

This is shaping up to be a great match, and he couldn't be happier. *I hope he's having a good time. He seems to be a little perplexed right now.* Those were Shelia's thoughts as she watched George's intensive stare out on the court. As the match played on he became reticent and this was a concern to her. As a third break approached, the score was 3-2, and with Juan in the lead. She then had to ask him "is everything okay?"

"Everything is great!" He said with excitement that surprised her.

Not wanting to pry too deep with questions about why he looked marginally angry at times, she just decided that for the moment his answer would have to do. As soon as that idea passed through her mind, she noticed him smiling intensely at something. *I probably should ask him what's made him so happy. Okay, she goes...* "George, what's...?"

Then just like that he interrupted her and said "wow, I was so right. I thought that's what he was doing."

Shelia wasn't sure if he was talking out loud or to her. After things had settled down, she asked him probably the question he had wanted her to ask. "Tell me," she said, "what was he doing and who are we talking about?"

With some time before the last break of the third set, he was eager to answer her. "I was wondering what Juan was doing in that second set. I wasn't sure why he didn't seem to be playing as hard as he did in the first one. Sorry dear, are you following me?"

Shelia had played tennis in college and was pretty good, so she was picking up on what he was saying when she replied "aw I was wondering what he was doing losing that set. He was letting Nadal use up his energy, and now it looks like he will win this third set easily at 6-2."

Having someone that you love and adore to share your passions on the same level is something to cherish. Leaning over towards her, he put his hand behind her head, and then pulled her closer for a kiss. Afterward, he said, "you are my angel from heaven; now let's watch this fourth set because it's going to be a doozy."

"Now, that was some kiss to follow up with your tennis statement. I guess I'll have to accept the whole thing."

George was speechless he thought of how to answer that, but no ideas came up. The match continued to follow what they both suspected and Juan Del Porto won the fourth set with an 8-6 tiebreaker. In no hurry, they stayed on about forty-five minutes and left to find somewhere to have dinner. This wasn't an easy task to do since all the restaurants near the stadium were full. George and Shelia decided to grab something light to eat and then took a train back to their home.

On the train, they were so tired, even though the ride was less than an hour George decided to ask for some dinner. Walking back to the restroom Shelia noticed how empty their car was until she spotted a little girl. She was all alone, appeared to be scared, and crying. Finding a seat right next to her Shelia said "dis-moi pourquoitupleures." *tell me why you are crying.*

"Je suissupposémonterce train pour être avec ma mère et j'ai peur d'être seul." *I'm supposed to ride on this train to be with my mom and I'm afraid to be alone.*

Shelia told her to wait right there until she returned from the ladies room. After she had finished, she collected the little girl, and took her to her seat. After an introduction to George, this sweet little girl ate some cookies and milk, and then fell asleep, and thirty-five minutes later they arrived at their destination. Walking down the steps with them, the little girl spotted her mom, and then took off.

She looked at him and said "well, George sometimes it is better that the rewards for doing something good are just stored in heaven."

He put his arm around her shoulder then replied "true, so true my dear."

Walking from the station, the two had a very eventful day. They talked about the little girl and how sweet she was. George admired how Shelia took her and made sure she was safe, but in his heart, he wasn't surprised because she was a great mom. *Too bad we didn't meet so many years ago* were his thoughts.

That evening before they turned in, George told Shelia the story of his first love, and how after her loss set him on a downward-spin. This was a very good discussion in that it helped her to understand that we all have hard times and we all come back from them. Shelia was so sad about what had happened to his mom and fiancé. Wondering if she hadn't gotten a divorce and moved to Three Rivers if they would have ever met?

They had a restful sleep, even with some snoring, caused them to wake up late. This was the first time that she was up before him, but it didn't take him long to smell the coffee and go downstairs. They had another morning working together in the kitchen then off to the beach to relax.

They spent some time visiting the friends they had made locally. That day on the pier they ran into an elderly couple that they had found there before. This lovely couple possessed valuable information, so Shelia shared a concern that she had about George losing his first love, and if she could ever take her place. They both talked with them about that and put that concern to rest when George confirmed that Shelia held a very special place in his heart.

CHAPTER 24

Blended is a good word to describe how well George was with Shelia's children. Over time he became so close to the kids that they asked if he wanted to adopt them as his own and with absolutely no contact from their biological dad Jake, he didn't see any problem with that now. George did everything that a loving daddy would do for his children. He was there for them through their trials and tribulations of becoming adults.

George worked with his friend Calvin on their new knee designs. At first, they were going to sell their designs until one of the large companies made them a favorable offer. They were given a yearly budget to hire a research and development team. Besides they were given an allowance for a facility to rent. The first thing George and Calvin did was to hire a financial advisor to handle the budget. The one thing that the large orthopedic manufacturing company got was all the copyrights to their designs.

Living in the lake house was a very special place. Calvin convinced his fiancé to have their wedding there, especially since Chicago wasn't that far away. They called their research and development company No Borders Medical Devices in honor of the Doctors without Borders where they met on tour. Their company was located in South Bend, Indiana to help recruit Notre Dame graduates. After a few years had gone by there were some problems to deal with from time to time.

Shelia would see one of the bridges and remember that his commitment was as strong as a bridge. Another time George took Steven to one of the bridges in Three Rivers and explained that even though he might not be there to help him, he would always be there to give him the tools he would need to handle problems in life. On that bridge he told Steven "look at this bridge we are on. Trucks with heavy loads drive over it, cold winds blow on it constantly, and the other aspects of the weather try to destroy it. The one constant is that it always stands, and yes it does receive some maintenance to help it survive. Look at this bridge and know that as long as I'm alive and capable I will always be there to help you my son."

Steven grew to be a fine young man who made

good grades, excelled in sports like golf, tennis, and swimming. Sweet little Julie as well made excellent grades and was certainly on her way to being the valedictorian of her class one day. Shelia went on later to form her practice and during this time she helped support her friend Susan to become a medical doctor like herself and Susan's husband John.

They once experienced some trouble when they were traveling the world as a family. It was Steven's senior year, and they decided to visit the United Kingdom using a chartered flight, and they landed at a small airport in Scotland. In the United Kingdom, all went well, with a few days visiting the castles. The next trip was to travel by boat down to England and watch a couple of matches at Wimbledon. George always tried to watch a tennis match wherever they traveled. They were in England for a week, seeing all the history around, but knowing that one week couldn't do justice to this historic land.

All was well when they drove over to Ireland, up the coast to Durbin. Riding in one of the boats, the weather was wet, and very windy. Julie and Shelia were waiting in the car because it was too nasty out there for them. George was walking along the dock with Steven when he noticed something interesting. The boards on the dock were very rickety and in need of repair, so George told Steven to go back for fear of the instability of the pier, and Steven returned to the cable stone sidewalk.

Turning around, walking back to the car, Steven just stopped. George didn't notice at first until he turned around to say something to him. He noticed that he wasn't there, so he looked back to find him lying on the ground almost motionless. Walking quickly back to him, he turned him over, picked up his head, then tried to communicate with him. His face looked pale, paler than from the cold weather. George noticed he was still breathing, but didn't notice any blood or broken bones, so he picked him up, and carried him to the car. They asked him what was wrong and George said "I don't know."

They called the local 911 number, and within five minutes an ambulance arrived. The medics examined him and then they put in a couple of needles. When he was all wrapped up on the gurney, they then put him in the van. George put the rental car in gear and followed the ambulance to the hospital. With Shelia and Julie both crying all the way to the hospital, George didn't want to stop them, he felt it would be better if they got that out of the way. George's thoughts were; *why are they crying so much? It could be that nothing bad is wrong with him after all, Shelia and I are doctors. One thing we've been taught is not to assume anything.*

Steven was taken into the emergency room on the same gurney he was transported on. George parked in the first spot he could find. Knowing that Shelia was so worried, he made sure to be on top of the situation.

What situation you might ask, well he knew that she would go up to the nurse's station, and bombard them with questions. Not to mention that she would tell them over and over that she was a family doctor, thinking that would give her access to all the information before the doctors had assessed it. George could sense that it was time to take charge because he could see that she's about to make her move.

"George, would you stay here with Julie? I need to go ask the nurses a couple of questions."

He walked up to her, put his arms around her, and said "my dear, let's sit here and wait for the doctor to come out."

"But George, I need to find out what's happening with my baby boy."

A compromise was the answer to this problem, and when he took her hand, George said "Julie come with us." She stood up, took her mom's hand, and then he said "let's go girls" and off they went to the nurse's station together.

Before the nurse could go down the hallway to find out more, one of the doctors walked up with information to tell them about their young man. Patiently they looked at her and waited for her to tell them what was wrong with Steven. She did not know that they were doctors, so she first looked at the chart, and then looked at them. Before the words formed into her mouth, Shelia said "we are both medical doctors so please tell us what is wrong with him."

She then told them something in medical terms that meant a snake bit him, but the poison didn't travel far enough because of the cold weather. He went into shock, so he went still, and was in a mild coma. Once he was given the antidote and some glucose, they then let him sleep. The doctor told them that he needed to sleep it off and the following day he would be fine, they only needed to monitor his blood.

Home, wonderful home, she thought how much she had missed it. The scare over Steven being bitten by a snake in Ireland was a lot. *Home, I missed you so much* again was Shelia's thought and now for some action! Unloading the vehicle as fast as they could, they all were happy. Steven was a bit tired after the accident, but all in all, he was fine. The first thing on Shelia's mind was to protect the family from snakes.

She went into full gear studying all she could about the snakes in their neck of the woods. Within two weeks she had purchased all kinds of paraphernalia to do with ridding your yard of snakes. On one occasion she talked with George about adopting some cats, many cats, but only for the yard. That's when he got suspicious and asked her why she wanted so many cats?

Her reply was a shock when she said "to help eliminate any snakes in our yard."

Assessing what she was doing, George came up with a plan, an old plan, but a good one, no doubt. He was able to convince her to wait until the weekend to look at cats for their yard. In the meantime, it was Wednesday, which was one of her days off, so it was time to take her to town. She hadn't driven the car with the top down at all that spring, and fortunately, the weather was nice, partly sunny with a temperature of 68. In the car and ready to go, he put their picnic basket in the back seat.

"George, what park will we be going to today?"

"I was thinking the one by the St. Joseph River would be nice."

Driving over the bridge, he gathered his thoughts of what he was going to tell her. No spaces were close to the bridge, but then again he hadn't mentioned to her that he was taking her to it after lunch. Sitting there waiting for her to arrange the plates his thoughts were; *okay she is going overboard with this snake phobia thing. I remember when mom took me here to help when I was stung by a bee. She explained how important bees were. She told me that if I were to treat them with love and respect, they would take care of our flowers by pollinating them.*

Lunch was perfect, just to be alone with the one you love, and on a special day like today. All their stuff was cleaned up and in the trash or the picnic basket. As always, they went for a walk around the park, but only across a bridge if George needed to impart some knowledge. He took her hand, and they strolled around the park very slowly along the river bank. The river was flowing nicely that day, without a lot of garbage in it, which always made George happy to see the beauty of his hometown.

Before they went back to pick up the basket, he turned her toward the bridge, and she thought *what's up, why is he taking me to the bridge?* Well, he walked her across to the middle where he stopped, put his arm around her waist then gave her a gentle hug, and a kiss on the head. He talked with her about what happened to Steven in Ireland. There were no arguments, she just acknowledged that he was fine, and as always everything works out for good to them who love.

Here's what he said "my dear, you are one of the most caring, loving, and hopeful people that I've ever known."

"Thank you dear you are the man of my dreams."

"Okay, I want you to think about how long this bridge has been here? Unless there is a plan to take it down by man or nature, it will be here for us. Steven had a snake bite, but he didn't die because it wasn't his time to. There is nothing we can do to prevent anyone from dying when their time comes. We live in the Midwest where we get snow at least three months out of the year, and all snakes leave until spring. Let's not go out of our way to try and alter any plans nature might have for them. Common sense is all we need to follow. Now the next time you feel fearful of something think of this bridge and how destiny controls it like everything else."

CHAPTER 25

Empty nesters, that is what they call you when the children are grown and possibly on their own. Either way, George and Shelia are for once in their marriage free, and all by themselves.

Julie was following in her parents' footsteps and would attend Notre Dame in the fall. Steven decided to put full-time college off for four years. He was in his third year in the Air Force. Also, he had been attending part-time classes at the community college for over a year, and was on schedule to have his two-year degree before his enlistment was over. Steven liked being stationed at Johnson AFB in North Carolina. On some weekends he would visit his uncle Peter, Aunt Betty, and his cousins. When Steven visited he would go fishing with all of them, yes Peter's family loved fishing, and his boat could hold them all.

All in all the Esperanza family had done very well. With Julie in her first year at Notre Dame, Steven was coming home, but not sure yet what he wanted to do. Financially they were doing great, that is without counting any money from Shelia's inheritance. While at work, George had been talking with Calvin about their time spent many years ago in Africa. Over the years, they kept contact with camp Peacock, and the volunteers running it.

He was not restless, he would think to himself; *do I continue to work with my company? I've enjoyed making better products for the orthopedic industry to use. Am I ready to go back and do something I loved so much, that brought me back from a tragedy? Maybe this is a time to discuss that with Shelia?*

It was a Sunday, and they were sitting on the back porch talking. Most of their conversation was about how great Julie was doing in school. Then it changed and turned to the fact that Steven was coming home soon. With some things still up in the air, George's thoughts were; *maybe this isn't a good time to talk about Africa?*

Decisions needed to be made now that Julie was doing her residency at her mom's practice. Shelia picked her but decided it would be better if one of her other doctors did the mentoring. Steven bummed around Europe for about a year then came home. In the Air Force Steven was in the engineering department and graduated with an AAS degree in mechanical design technology. He wasn't ready to go back to college then but wanted to do some computer design work. He was qualified in design engineering from working with his dad, in the Air Force, and in college. Calvin quickly hired him as a CAD designer in their R and D engineering department. It looked like the children were set, plus Steven was fine living at home until things changed.

Their Grandma had passed away two years back, and that day was her anniversary. There were times since then that Shelia felt her presence more than ever. Alone in the kitchen this bright morning, she was so grateful for the many things she had. While rolling some dough for pie crusts, she remembered about her mom showing her how to do it when she was a teenager. Smelling the dough, and holding the roller in her hand her thoughts were; *never had I thought this day would come. Not that I'm not grateful because I am, I can't shake the thought of missing you. Mom I know you're here to see how wonderful everything has turned out.* She hugged herself as if it was her mom doing it and then put the pies in the oven.

She has no idea of what I'm thinking, so I have to find a way to start this conversation about Calvin gently, and I want to do another tour in Africa. George was contemplating how to run this thought by her that day. Then as he tossed his line in the water, he looked behind him to where Steven was fishing too. "Steven," he said.

"Yes, dad, what's up?"

"Good question, I want to run something by you before I talk to your mom."

"Okay dad, shoot."

"First off I want to tell you how happy I am that you are home and working at our company doing CAD design. I know Calvin likes having you in engineering and you are doing a great job..."

"Dad that's not the question you want to talk to mom about."

"You're right, here it is, Calvin and I have been talking about going back overseas to Africa again. The terms are for two years each and I don't want to be away from your mom, but we want to do one more stint over there. It's been many years and we aren't getting any younger."

He thought about what his dad had said and thought about it some more. Reeling his line in, he sighed and said "dad, this is a tough one. The only thing I can come up with is this; if you are serious about going, then the best thing to do would be to take her to one of the bridges, where you can assure her that it will be alright."

"Son, I guess you see that life isn't that easy. I will do just that. You know the bridges have never let me down before." With him concurring with Steven, they went back to fishing. That day they brought fish home to clean, and eat later. There were no stories about fishing though, George never liked them, and Steven agreed.

Bridges of Three Rivers

Courage was nothing that George had to muster up, but that day was different. He wanted to do this very much. It seemed like this was what was next in his life, but he didn't want to be away from her for two years! *Think, think, think,* were the thoughts that raced across his mind, and then a laugh when he remembered that, that was a line from Winnie the Pooh Tigger movie. *Here she comes, I think I'm ready, I know I'm ready.* "Darling, do you want to go for a picnic today?"

"Sure, when do you want to go?"

"Oh, I don't know, we will need to put something together to eat."

"Then get your butt in the kitchen and help me right now."

"I'm sorry, I was daydreaming."

They made lunch, packed it in the basket, loaded in the car, and off they went into town. This day was a little gloomy, cool, and windy. He pulled into the park and said "let's eat in the car today."

"Good idea," she said with a chuckle.

They enjoyed good food, lots of coffee, but not too much coffee, after all they were away from home. While finishing his sandwich George told her "let's go for a walk."

"Sure, give me a couple of minutes to finish this carrot."

Thinking they were going around the park, she was surprised when he turned her towards the bridge.

She asked "why are we going to the bridge?"

"Because I have something I want to talk with you about."

"Oh no, did something bad happen?"

He stopped, turned to face her, put his hands on her shoulders, and said "no, nothing is wrong. I just have something to ask you."

She then kissed him and they walked on to the top of the bridge. Then he said "I don't know how to say this, but here it goes. Calvin and I have been talking about going back to Africa one more time."

There was silence between them, she stood there, not angry or sad, but almost numb. He was afraid that she would cry, yell, or even worse, run away! He was tongue tied, and his thoughts were; *oh my God, what have I done? She knows that these are two-year commitments. Geez, is she thinking how selfish I must be for wanting to leave her to go off and live in abject poverty for two years? Please, please, understand.* He then stopped his thoughts and said "dear, what do you think? Are you okay?"

Seeing how worried he was, she laughed and said "can I go too? After all, I am also a medical doctor."

From the intensity of his laughter she thought he was crazy. I mean he just kept laughing. She started to walk away until he said "damn it, why didn't I think about that! If you were to go that would make me so happy." Then he grabbed her, hugged her and squeezed her, but didn't call her George, because that was his name.

Calvin was ecstatic. Although he had different news; his wife put her foot down. She let him know that their children were too young for him to be traipsing off to Africa for two years. Either way, Calvin was very happy that Shelia was going with George instead. He confirmed with George about the dangers and that they should make sure their will was up to date before they left. The kids were surprised; at least Julie was since Steven already knew. They planned to spend the next six months getting their bodies, finances, and family in order before leaving.

Shelia was so excited to be traveling with him because he talked about this tour when they met. Later after they were married, he told her how this commitment of helping people helped him through a very rough time, especially after he lost his wife, mother, and their first child on the road that tragic night. To go with him was something she thought about but it never came up. Life was certainly about to change again for these two.

Working out was great, they would jog around the lake, swim, chop wood for the winter, and volunteer with Habitat for Humanity building homes. Before leaving they were able to meet Steven's new girlfriend that he had met while at work. She was a vendor that showed up one day to talk about some computer software, and her name was Carol. Although Steven wasn't the expert on this subject, she caught his eyes. After Carol had left he talked with the IT girl about who she was and if she would return. It just so happened, that she had a return date to test the software that they had installed. Steven made sure he was involved in this and asked her to go to lunch with him. He turned on the charm, made another date with her, then they hit it off, and have been seeing each other for a few months.

Julie was not looking to meet anyone although she had many friends, but was too intent on gaining her medical practice first. Her mom was very happy with her progress, and after all, she was following in her footsteps. They would spend lunches together when their schedules were open. She was sad that her mom was going away, and she was worried that something bad could happen to her over there, but then she remembered the bridges.

She took Julie to the bridges of Three Rivers several times during the six month period before they left for Africa. The time was well spent reminding her of all the examples that George shared with her over the years. Those bridges were the focal points for the Esperanza family all these years. Steven received the same treatment from George who had taken him there to learn all those secrets too.

Steven drove them to South Bend to take the train to Chicago and then fly overseas for two long years. Very quiet, they were both in the driver's and passenger's seats, with their parents in the back. With no music in the car, George tried to start a conversation, but they were too sad to talk. Shelia was sitting there lost in her thoughts which were; *I'm looking at this being a critical time in my life. To do something like this for no rewards other than to fill your heart with love is so meaningful that I pray I am given the strength to accomplish it.*

The humming of the road seemed to put George and Shelia to sleep. They were both aware of the tiring journey ahead. Steven and Julie noticed they were asleep. Had she been crying? He noticed and said "yes sis' I know I'm sad too, but our parents are very good people."

"I know Steven, I'm so proud of them, but I can't help but be afraid."

He smiled, then had a low chuckle, and said "do we need to go to the bridges while they are gone?"

That made her feel better, and she said "that would be a good thing to do during the next two years."

While entering South Bend, Steven said, "Wake up sleepy heads."

Shortly after Steven had said that they were there and unloaded their two small travel bags. With hugs and kisses, they said their goodbyes, and then left for this last adventure.

CHAPTER 26

Hot, dry, and miserable, that was all she could think about. She wasn't about to complain to him because she had all those examples of the three bridges to fall back on. *He would have taken me back home if he knew I didn't like it here. Right now I'm not happy, but I will push through.* It would take some time for Shelia to get used to this place, but her determination would certainly win out.

There was excitement he hadn't felt in a long time, but there were also many dangers that he made her aware of. Each time he went into detail about the battles with the warlords, he waited for her to change her mind. He was surprised because the worse the stories became, the stronger her desire to go grew. *Who is this woman, she has never done anything like this before? Could it be that this is just a false sense of courage talking on her behalf? I mean when the shit hits the fan, I hope she doesn't flip out on me.* George was perplexed and wanted nothing more than for her attitude to carry on.

The first week at camp Peacock he was so happy to be back, and although there were no familiar faces in the camp, he was sure that he would remember one or two in the village. On day four, the processing was done, and they were going on their way to the village to perform medical treatments. Equipped with some old army vehicles that had been restored to good as new condition, Shelia was excited to ride on them after departing from the plane that day to arrive at the village.

These precious little children, she had never seen people in such poverty before, something a wealthy girl like her would not have seen. Her heart broke many times that day, watching these people walking up, looking for help *if only I could spend all my family money to help them.* Her thoughts were so single-minded that day as her second mind was so silent it could as well be dead. When a mom brought her little two-year-old girl up to her, Shelia couldn't help but put this tiny little angel in her arms and then cry.

George was back in the swing of things and you would not have known that he'd been gone over fifteen years. He took on the patients that needed orthopedic services. This was a perfect opportunity for him to work with the orthopedic companies back home by having them send him some supplies. The company that he and Calvin started had been supplying camp Peacock for over ten years now. Before leaving, he also received some great assistance from his local lodge brothers. They took up a collection which totaled approximately $21,254, which he had put in with a fund for Steven to use to send them supplies when requested.

Julie was a writer as well as a medical student. Each week, she would send her parents a letter talking about her week in school. In her letters she'd ask them to also write in detail about each week there. During this time, Shelia started writing a journal of their time spent in Africa. This went on for the entire time there and later would become a novel.

Always tested by these thugs, those were George's thoughts because he never forgot how they would drive into the village, and take from the people all the supplies they had given them. It hadn't happened, but he wished there was some Rambo to come over and help them. He almost convinced Peter to join them, but couldn't bear something happening to his little brother.

Halfway between the camp and the village is where they came out. Driving very fast behind them were the warlords along with their thugs. This brought back memories where he remembered how it all broke down to logistics like fuel, distance, speed, ammo, and the Calvary from the camp. Also he noticed that these engagements they had were almost textbook. They would leave the village then on their way back to their camp is when these warlords would chase them. Sometimes they got close, but the doctors were always saved at the last minute.

Shelia was frightened the first couple of times, and after that, she had respect for the circumstances. They were never a dime a dozen, or even old hat, not when your life was on the line. However, she gained more and more confidence in their ability to fend them off. A couple of nights after a chase, she and George would enjoy some of the best sex they could ever remember. I suppose that adrenaline had to be let out somewhere.

Being grateful, and feeling like twenty-year-olds they had responsibilities yes, but they hadn't felt this free in a long time. A few months out of each year the two would work in the garden planting vegetables then months later picking them when needed. The camp was a fully sustained community that not only took care of itself, but helped the locals learn how to do the same. Camp Peacock had been instrumental in the local village's growth over the years.

Time spent helping and getting to know the people was always her favorite thing to do and George enjoyed the satisfaction he gained from helping those people that had nothing to give in return except gratitude. *This kind of experience was something a lot of people needed to know* George thought while he hung some white clothes out on a clothesline. They usually had servants do that for them, not in a servitude manner, but more so like a job.

Steven and Julie were so proud of their parents that they would send them gifts once a month. Steven was still dating Carol, and their relationship was getting more and more serious. Julie was still working at Shelia's practice and learning a lot of good things.

Calvin's daughter was starting to become interested in her daddy's company's work. She was thirteen years old and liked hanging around the office after school. One day Steven was eating his lunch at work with Carol where she spotted Calvin's daughter Lilly sitting alone, so she invited her to sit with them. She and Steven liked Lilly, so they volunteered to mentor her in the work that each one did.

Steven wrote all about this in the family letter, Julie continued to update them on her weekly progress, and they wrote about how much they missed them. Sometimes time went by fast, their Children's letters were a blessing, they made them happy, and at the same time sad. Understanding what they were doing and how important it was only helped to strengthen their resolve. They were treating the sick, helping teach in their schools, building more homes, and then came the regular work around the camp too.

George built another gin still which he made sure to take a picture to send back to Calvin. Shelia took some time to acquire a taste for it, but after being chased by bandits across the desert a few times, she found it to be very satisfying. Wherever one went, you could find the other, except one place, but that's probably a good thing for each. They were settled in, their tent was not too big, maybe a medium in size.

Reading the letters from home caused their hearts to wander off from missing all the excitement of Steven dating, Julie becoming a doctor, and spending time on the bridges. Most nights they were too tired to do anything but sit in their tent, drink gin, and talk about raising the children or their work back home. Lost in this nostalgia, George couldn't understand why they just seemed to be numb emotionally.

Once, this malaise caught up with them to the point of their danger! It happened in the village when they were doing their routine check-ups. Sure, their hearts were always open for these people, and they acknowledged the little ones with their troubles. All those feelings seemed to be handled by their subconscious minds. Not aware of that, they just carried on with their work.

George was the doctor in charge that day: it was his responsibility to ensure everything was done on time and per the schedule. What this meant was that he needed to make sure they wrapped everything up before it got dark. Doing that helped to protect them and the villagers from the warlords. These warlords would come in after the sunset, and if any villagers were out then, they would kill them. The doctors needed to be on the road in time for the logistical elements to work.

He took on another patient when it was already past the stopping point. It wasn't pleasant, but the people would need to wait one more day, or there could be hell to pay. Feeling that something was wrong Shelia looked over at him, then he noticed her, and then she asked "shouldn't we be loading up by now to go back?"

He didn't mean to ignore her, but he was engrossed in fixing his patient. His nurse heard her and answered "Dr. Shelia, I believe you're right" then she nudged George.

"What?" He said, as he put down the instrument he was working with.

"We need to leave now doctor."

After noticing that Shelia was packing up and so was his nurse, he then kicked it into high gear stuffing the expensive things in the tackle boxes leaving the cotton balls and the other less costly things. They loaded them all up and told the people that they would be back in a couple of days and that they all needed to get back home quickly. They were able to fit the rest of the patients on one of the trucks and carry them to their homes. This wrecked the doctors' exit schedule, but they knew this needed to be done. I mean what good was it to take care of them only to allow the warlords to abuse them?

They, of course, made it back safely, but it was a close one. That night Shelia asked him what was wrong and what he thought could be their problem. The following day was their one day off during the week, so they spent a little extra time drinking gin that night with no more questions, just talking about home and the children. It didn't take too long before they were so tired that they were both out like a light.

He slept with the thought of her question on his mind; waking up bright and early the next morning, George had the answer. Lying there in bed his thoughts were; *she wanted to know why we seemed to be in a fog lately. Well, I think I know the answer. I'll get some coffee and bring her back a cup then we can discuss it.* With that thought he got up, got dressed, and then kissed her as he left to get coffee.

When he returned, she was awake, dressed, and waiting for him. As he entered with two cups of coffee, she said "you need that much caffeine, or you just want me to wake up?"

"Good question my dear, but I plan on answering your question from yesterday."

Smiling at him, she toasted her coffee cup and said "go ahead, Governor."

As they sat drinking their cups of coffee, he explained that they were spending too much time reminiscing about days gone by. Shelia understood, but wondered why they had started doing that? To get to the bottom of why he spent a lot of the time using the bridges as examples for understanding was on her mind. It wasn't that what they were talking about was negative; in fact, they were some very memorable times. What they didn't see was that when you talk about things that are in the past at night, especially right before you go to sleep, your subconscious mind will try to give you that again.

Knowing that that was nearly impossible, then that energy would have been wasted on things that couldn't materialize again. Therefore, anything new would be suppressed from happening. This is known as stagnation, and it chokes your Spirit from receiving new blessings.

Bridges of Three Rivers

CHAPTER 27

It was a new day in Africa for the Esperanza's because they were now back in control of their minds. Therefore, their surroundings would be controlled by the two masters. With no electronic devices for communication, there were no distractions, or however you would look at it. This allowed them to study more in the metaphysical and quantum physical world too. Their goal wasn't to become anything in particular, but to obtain better learning of their minds, and the energies around them.

They found a witch doctor and a soothsayer in the village. Some days they would have them visit the camp so that they could spend more hours with them. A lot of the information the Spiritual people would impart was quite useful in helping them make good decisions.

George and Shelia were free to explore a lot of things, so many things on their minds, from many years ago. Some days it just felt like they were in their twenties again, working hard, and playing hard. One thing for sure was that these two had found a new love in each other that they could never have imagined was even possible. If the two weren't so right for each other, then these conditions would certainly be their undoing.

They had now spent fourteen months in Africa, but who was counting anyway, both were not ready to leave, even with only ten months to go. Before their time was up they wanted to make sure nothing was left for them to do. Near death escapes were becoming more and more common, and it seemed the warlords were obtaining better equipment. These warlords were still hell-bent on obtaining some if not all the goods from camp Peacock.

These two were going on another trip back into the village for routine medical work. What they didn't know was that the warlords were waiting to seize the day and possibly conquer them. The only question was; could they still be ready to defend themselves from an enemy they had seen many times?

"Short timers" that was the name they were called, especially for the ones that were ex-military like George. Preparing for that mission wasn't any different than the others. However, that day was going to be one of their last ones, if not the last one! Shelia was ready even faster than she had been before. *It took her long enough to get the hang of this. I got it; we will go home take several months off then come back.* Those were George's thoughts, and he was excited about coming back again. He missed doing this, and he didn't realize just how much.

They were on their toes that day and cognizant of the fact that they would be going home in less than two weeks. The funny thing about their leaving was that in that part of the world you didn't exchange emails, phone numbers, or any other type of contact except for the ones in the camp. There weren't any means to contact the villagers, but only through the camp personnel. Shelia made a point to take plenty of pictures and write down their names. She planned on returning with George again shortly after some time at home.

On the truck, they were loaded and ready to go. The air was hot as always; the air was usually very dry, it seemed that part of the world would beg for some moisture. While riding along in the front of the third truck, Shelia's mind had some weird thoughts that day; *this reminds me of the first Star Wars movie, where Luke Skywalker was living on this planet. Wow, I can remember him going out and checking the moisture collectors. What a great memory that is. Today I will try my best to absorb as much of the goodness that is around me. These people rely on us so much, and it's good to see how they are growing in the ways of being more civilized.*

They arrived early that day in the village, so there weren't that many people lined up for help. But George wanted to set a record that day for the number of people they would attend to. He instructed one of the drivers to take a security guard with him and drive through the village. Their mission was to round up as many people that needed some medical attention as possible. This was a brilliant thing to do because it would have taken them longer to walk especially the ones that were physically challenged.

It was a madhouse that day; only three doctors were helping so many people. Their nurses would fill in and finish up some of the more basic jobs the doctors would perform. Shelia was in her groove; she couldn't believe that this was the way she could give back to this world. She and George weren't the kind of people that felt guilty about what they possessed. They weren't the opposite either; they were the type of people that were grateful for all their blessings. So even when they did things for charity's sake, they were even happier. Sometimes after doing good deeds for others, they thought that the pleasure they received in doing them was greater than the help the people received.

It was late midday, and they were taking a break from work. A tent had been erected to help block the blazing heat from the sun. Their food was minimal, but they drank plenty of water; they were cautious about dehydration. Knowing this, they planned on helping the ones that were there and sending the ones who were done home with a bottle of water. The engineers were doing great work in building the treatment plant and then training the locals on how to do the water purification.

There were many things to be proud of that day, and it was certainly a great realization. George thought; *how wonderful it is to find someone who shares your ambitions in life the way Shelia does.* With these thoughts going into that direction, he decided to let her know how he felt. It was not that he hadn't told her this before, but that day was a very special day for him. Holding her hand after eating his protein bar and taking the final swig of water, he said "my dear you are one of the most amazing women I've ever known."

"Well, thank you, dear, you inspire me to do so many things. When you invited me to come with you here to Africa, I was overwhelmed with pride that you considered me to do this type of work."

"Shelia, you raised two children all those years, put yourself through medical school, and then had the guts to travel across the country to find a better place for your family. I think that shows what you are capable of doing, this is just the crowning of your ability, and believe me, I've seen many fail at this."

Their time was up, and then they both headed back to the med area to work on more patients. There were still many more lined up, and George wasn't sure if they would get through them all that day. He pledged himself that he would finish the day with no people unattended. Sharing this goal with the rest of the team, they too committed to helping achieve that goal. As the day approached it's ending, they also noticed that the supplies were quickly running out. That meant that they would have to use less of them but still make sure the quality didn't diminish.

"Whew, that sure was a day of work," Shelia said as they noticed no one else in the line for help.

"Yes, and we did it! I can't wait to look at the numbers for today. Maybe we will have broken a record before we leave next week." George was looking around and then noticed some of the trucks were missing. He asked one of the drivers "why are some of the trucks gone?"

The driver said "they have taken the last lot of the patients back to the village."

Noticing that the sun was lower than the last time they were there. Which was only a couple of days earlier, George thought; *damn it, I might get all of us killed today. My ambition to always be better has to stop.* His heart was racing, and he knew it! That didn't prevent him from working like a madman to get everything loaded. Like several times before, he would leave some stuff, but fortunately that day he didn't have that problem because the supplies were practically all gone.

They were loaded up and now ready to pull out! Shelia was in charge that day, and thankfully she didn't panic. Once on the road she instructed the trucks to increase their speed by ten miles an hour. Doing some quick calculations, one of the engineers assured her that that would get them in on time. What they didn't know that day was that the warlords had a few surprises in store for them. One of those surprises was a vehicle that was equipped with a turbocharger.

Probably fifteen miles from the camp all was going as planned. That's when they spotted the dust clouds behind them! Not knowing if it was a dirt devil or a vehicle just meant that they didn't change anything. George noticed a worried look on her face and asked her "is everything okay?"

"I don't know, do you see the big dirt clouds behind us?"

"Yes, I do, do you think it could be the warlords?"

Shelia was now ready to take action; the next thing that she did was to alert the base that they would be going in at high speed. "Increase your speed another five miles an hour" she instructed all the vehicles. Keenly aware that if they were to go too fast, they would run the risk of overheating the trucks and no matter what they did, and one of the warlord's vehicles was catching up with them quickly. Another minute or two went by, and the bullets started to fly their way. You could see these rounds hit the ground behind them and kick up the dirt.

Never before had they been caught even after all these years. George thought that was a very impressive statistics to hold. Knowing that being caught would lead to being tortured and then killed wasn't one thing they wanted to break. He sometimes thought of the F-15 Fighting Eagle, probably one of the most impressive fighter aircraft ever made. Its distinction was that an American one had never been shot down in battle.

Loading up the machine guns and the other weapons they had was their primary task. The bullets were coming closer and closer, so they were very anxious to get back to the camp quickly. George radioed Shelia and asked her if they should go ahead and start firing back. When she received his words, she assessed the situation and asked him how far the bullets were coming to the last trucks? When he told her that they were hitting the bumper, she said "fire at will, George."

That's just what he did, being there were three in the back right behind them. George instructed them not to waste their ammo because he wasn't sure how long it would last. There was a problem though and that problem was their trucks were starting to overheat. With that happening, George made sure that the rounds they were sending at the approaching vehicle were aimed at the biggest part. With their trucks having to slow down, the other warlord vehicles started to catch up. This created a problem in that; the rounds were starting to come faster and more plentiful. So with that, he had another truck drop back to parallel them. In doing that he was able to bring in more firepower to slow down the warlords.

You could start to see the hill, and that was where you could see the camp. Shelia was so concerned with making sure the trucks didn't overheat. She felt confident that George would do what needed to be done to lay down firepower to subdue the warlords' advance.

On the radio, he called to give her an update. "We are taking in more fire from them and their vehicles are starting to catch up with us. Can we increase our speed?"

She replied "sorry George we are running these engines too hot as it is. I received word from the camp that the Calvary was dispatched some ten minutes ago and should be over the hill soon."

Going by her words, he knew that they only had a few rounds of ammunition at best so he implied an old tactic from way back. He instructed everyone with a weapon to line up, load up, and take aim. Once all were ready to fire, he then told them to fire as quickly as they could, therefore expended all their ammunition. While this was going on, the firepower they created caused their enemy to pull back to get away from the massive firepower. Then when George and his people ran out of ammo, the enemy started to come back with a vengeance.

Shelia radioed to George and quizzically asked "what now George?"

He said "good question" as the bullets started to reach their trucks.

A few evasive maneuvers weren't doing a lot of good to slow them down. Shelia was ready to give the order to increase their speed when they spotted the Calvary over the hill in front of them. The whole group yelled a thunderous cheer as the trucks went past them, circled back around then started shooting at the enemy until the warlords motioned for their trucks to breakaway and retreat. They tempted fate that day!

CHAPTER 28

They were waving goodbye to their driver below, then he just stopped, and all the while miles away their plane was still climbing up. When they left the camp to drive to the airport, they didn't see the warlords several miles away watching them. The gates opened then they took off with a few trucks behind to provide cover. Pulling away from the rear convoy, they proceeded onward to the airport.

That day there was a plane arriving that hadn't made the trip before and one thing they forgot to do was to scout the area before the plane landed. The warlords were able to eradicate the rear trucks, but since they were separated, the lead vehicle carrying George and Shelia did not know what was happening. Therefore, the warlords were then able to pass the rear trucks and then follow the others to the airport. Once they were near the airport, the warlords couldn't get any closer than half a mile because of the security, so they quickly unloaded their vehicles, then located the runway.

Seeing a plane taking off, the Marauders pulled out an RPG (Rocket Propelled Grenade) that they had purchased on the black market. And being so near the flight path of the plane they were able to target it while waiting for it to come into range. No one noticed them down there, and they had passed the truck below that the doctors were waiving at. George spotted the rocket's smoke trail, but it was too late to do any invasive maneuvers, plus he wasn't flying.

A very high pitched whistle followed! They looked that way and saw the rocket coming for the plane! In a flash, they saw it hit the side! It seemed like minutes, but it was only seconds, seconds that told a lifetime story. He looked at Shelia for the last time, no time to even say a complete word except maybe, SHIT! Then the sound of the rocket cut into the metal, hiss, and then boom! There was a very bright flash of light, probably temporarily blinding them, but of course, it didn't matter. The fire in their plane was so hot, so intense, and so oxygen-consuming.

Looking up from below, their comrades said that the left wing spun away on fire, and out of control. The fuselage was engulfed in flames, and turning down to the ground, and therefore didn't take long to find the earth! It was as if it was a massive piece of metal and the earth was a magnet. However, George would quickly tell you that that plane was made of aluminum and it was not magnetic. That is if he was able to speak.

"They were loved by many although not many people knew what they were doing. What can we say about them, a father, a mother, two doctors, and two very good friends to many people?" Calvin read the eulogy. Peter was supposed to do it but wanted Calvin to say some words since he and George had been to Africa before on such a mission. The children didn't know what to think; here they were grown up and only days away from seeing their parents after two long years. Instead, they were now at their funeral, and it was not what they expected at all.

Julie had a lot to tell her mom, but there was one thing that she kept as a surprise. That surprise was that she had met a man that she hadn't even told her mom about. It had happened about two weeks before they were to leave from Africa. *Why didn't I tell them before, now it's too late? Now I feel terrible, really terrible.* These were her thoughts at the funeral and although she was crying it wasn't only for their deaths, but that she hadn't communicated with them in a few weeks. What was so weird was that she normally wrote them one letter per week; she decided that since they were coming home that a letter would not be received in time, and her letter would bounce around the globe looking for them.

Steven saw his sister cry but noticed her boyfriend with his arm around her in a soft consoling mode. He was content to let him do his due diligence, except that he walked over to her, and said "sis, it's going to be fine, they will always reside in our hearts."

Many people were there for this sad and happy occasion. This was not made more apparent until Dr. Fritz stood up to say some words. Her speech was very uplifting, and in it, she described how these two medical doctors were just angels disguised as humans. The things she said would normally be taken as a metaphor but the words she used, and the way she organized them, the people there believed she was right.

The eulogy that Calvin read was not very long, and he wasn't up for speaking. He did this for the memory of his friend that he had always thought of as a brother. In his heart, all he could think about was how he was going to do his best to make sure that Julie and Steven were taken care of? Peter flew in a couple of days before to help the children with all the arrangements.

This day was a very sad one for Peter, the memories that swirled in his mind were; *my brother, a good man who lost his first love, our mother, and a first child that was on the way, all on the same day.* On seeing Calvin there, he walked over to him, put his arms around him, and cried. Calvin wasn't able to shed any more tears, so he padded Peter on the back and said:

"my brother, we will certainly miss him, we will certainly miss him."

Steven remembered Jenny in Seattle, looked her up and gave her the sad news. Jenny was heartbroken but still managed to fly there for the funeral. When she arrived the day before the ceremony, she immediately put her arms around Steven and Julie. To her, they were like her children from the standpoint of being their parent for a short time. Julie thought of her as her mom and this made Jenny feel so happy. The funeral was a big event; probably more than one hundred people were in attendance, and only one was a sibling or thereabouts in the family lineage.

Shelia and George lived their lives in the best way they could, always eager to learn all the wonderful ways that brought good, and always ready to help all around them. I would like to close their story with this poem.

Bridges

Life in this form is not to be taken lightly so know.
That it will only last as long as this form will grow.
It's not to be thought of as merely a game.
Live consciously, love all, and find no blame.

Like the bridges that are built to carry a load.
Build your character to leave stories to be told.
To understand that this time is just an illusion.
It helps you to push on through life's confusion.

Our Spirits love this dimensional connection.
Good and bad will come to provide reflection.
Feel the experiences to the fullest and do believe.
All things pass away so don't let them deceive.

Remember we are all one from the great Source.
Before we took this form we did plan our course.
While you are here look to the structures very clear.
They are built to help us when darkness brings fear.

Master Buddha said that the jar fills drop by drop.
Make sure to do the little things and reach the top.
A bridge won't last forever, this is an undeniable fact.
Follow your heart and know there is nothing you lack!